“It’s *oll recht.*” Silas re
put a big, calloused h
“I understand.”

Warmth ran through Mary from the gentle touch. If she could just let go and trust him… She had never experienced that kind of security before. But it was too soon to let down her guard. She needed to stay strong.

“What we’re doing is unusual,” Silas continued. His eyes remained on hers, steady and reassuring. “Folks might talk. They might even say we shouldn’t go through with it.”

“*Ya.* They might. And I don’t want to let them down.”

Silas stared at her, as if trying to figure her out. “I don’t think you could do that if you tried.”

Mary gave a little laugh and looked away. “You don’t know me yet.”

Silas paused, then said, “Let’s go meet that bishop of yours. I’ll help you face it.”

Mary swallowed hard and met his gaze. “You will?”

“For certain sure. We’re going to be married, aren’t we? I figure this is my problem as much as yours.”

After **Virginia Wise**'s oldest son left for college and her youngest son began high school, she finally had time to pursue her dream of writing novels. Virginia dusted off the keyboard she once used as a magazine editor and journalist to create a world that combines her love of romance, family and Plain living. Virginia loves to wander Lancaster County's Amish country to find inspiration for her next novel. While home in Northern Virginia, she enjoys painting, embroidery, taking long walks in the woods, and spending time with family, friends and her husband of almost twenty-five years.

Books by Virginia Wise

Love Inspired

An Amish Christmas Inheritance
The Secret Amish Admirer
Healed by the Amish Nanny
A Home for His Amish Children

Visit the Author Profile page
at LoveInspired.com for more titles.

A HOME FOR HIS AMISH CHILDREN

VIRGINIA WISE

LOVE INSPIRED
INSPIRATIONAL ROMANCE

LOVE INSPIRED®
INSPIRATIONAL ROMANCE

ISBN-13: 978-1-335-90472-0

A Home for His Amish Children

Love Inspired
22 Adelaide St. West, 41st Floor
Toronto, Ontario M5H 4E3, Canada
www.LoveInspired.com

Printed in U.S.A.

There is no fear in love;
but perfect love casteth out fear.
—1 John 4:18

To my friend Dana,
whom I can always count on for advice.

Chapter One

Mary King had never done anything out of the ordinary before. She was careful to fit in and please everyone. She lived a good, Plain life, tried to follow every rule, and meet every expectation. So it seemed impossible that she was standing at the living-room window of her little white clapboard house, peering into a swirl of snow, anxiously waiting for the man she would marry to arrive.

A man she had never met before.

None of Mary's friends or family could have dreamed that she was capable of such an extraordinary plan. Then again, no one knew how desperate she had become.

Mary wiped the fog her breath made on the windowpane, then ran her fingers across her crisply starched apron and *kapp*, checking and rechecking that everything was in place. She wanted everything to be perfect when this stranger arrived with his two motherless children. Her mind raced with thoughts of what his first impression of her might be. Would he be relieved? Disappointed? What if he was so crest-fallen at the sight of her that he turned on his heel and stormed away without even saying hello?

At thirty-four years old, Mary had already been overlooked by the men who lived in Bluebird Hills, her little Amish community that was nestled in the green fields and farmland of Lancaster County, Pennsylvania. She had waited and waited for love, but the years had rolled by, until she was past the age that an Amish woman could expect a proposal. She had given up hope of ever having a family of her own. After a lifetime of rejection, it was hard to believe that this stranger would want to go through with the match after meeting her.

As Mary strained to see the hired car coming down the road from the bus station, she wondered what a man like Silas Hochstetler would look like and how he would act. Would he be quiet and reserved, or loud and boisterous? Would he be thoughtful and considerate? Mary turned away from the window, then immediately spun back around. She couldn't leave her post, not even for an instant. She couldn't bear to miss the exact moment he appeared.

Then she heard the low rumble of a car in the distance. Mary leaned into the window until her nose bumped the cold glass, as a blue sedan appeared through the swirling snow. Her heart thudded in her chest as she watched the car slowly make its way down the wintry road, its windshield wipers going full speed to clear the heavy, wet snowflakes. She took a deep breath, smoothed her apron one last time and marched to the front door.

Mary flung open the door to see a man emerging from the hired car. His back was to her as he paid the *Englisch* driver through the passenger window. Her stomach turned somersaults as she waited to see his face. She gripped the edge of the doorjamb, debating whether or not to go toward him. Would she seem too eager if she hurried to greet him? Would she appear too disinterested if she stayed where she was, hovering in the doorway? She didn't know what to do, so she just stood and stared, completely and utterly unsure of herself.

The man waved to the *Englisch* driver and finally turned around. Mary inhaled sharply. He was tall with a good, honest face and strong, broad shoulders. His brown eyes were kind, but sad. Mary sensed there was both love and pain behind them.

He was not smiling and Mary wondered

what he was thinking. He caught her eye and nodded as two children reluctantly slipped out of the back seat to stand on the curb beside him. The skinny little boy had brown hair and brown eyes, like his father, and looked painfully shy as he reached for Silas's hand and clung to it. The lost-looking teenage girl hung back from her brother and father, clutching her bag to her chest, the expression on her face achingly defensive. She would have been pretty, with her dark blond hair, big brown eyes and button nose, if her face had not been pulled into a frown.

Mary felt a confusing contradiction of emotions. Her heart warmed at the thought of forming a family with this man and these children whose needs were as desperate as hers. And yet, they stared at her with such distrust in their eyes that she feared they would never let her into their hearts.

Silas said something to his children that Mary couldn't hear. They responded in whispers as they stared at Mary with questioning eyes from across her front yard. Silas's expression tightened as he began to walk toward her. She watched as he strode up the stone pathway, past the row of snowcapped maple trees and the neatly trimmed boxwoods that lined her narrow front porch, and up the steps. His children hung back and, for a moment, it was just the two of them, staring at each another. He was even taller than she had realized and she had to tilt her head up to look into his face. Mary's knees felt weak and her pulse pounded in her ears as she fell into the dark pools of his eyes. Her mouth opened, then closed again. She had so much to say that she couldn't say anything at all. After so many years of waiting and hoping, her future husband stood before her and the wonder of that zipped through her like electricity.

"Mary King?" Silas asked after a moment. His voice was deep and rich, and Mary liked it immediately. A moment passed before he frowned and repeated, "Mary King?"

"Ya." Mary felt her cheeks flush hot and red with embarrassment. She had been so overwhelmed by the moment that she had not responded the first time he asked. *How foolish I must seem!* she thought. She cleared her throat and looked down. "That's me."

Silas stood on the porch, studying her. The snowflakes on his cheeks and beard began to melt and he wiped his face with the sleeve of his black coat. "Can, uh… can we *kumme* in?"

Mary flinched inside. "*Ya*, *ya*, of course. I'm sorry. I didn't mean to leave you standing there…" She silently berated herself. How could she expect Silas to go through with their arranged marriage when she couldn't even manage to ask him to come in from the snow? What must he think of her?

She stepped back to let him inside her warm, cozy living room. Woodsmoke drifted past her, through the open door, and rose into the cold, winter sky. Silas glanced back and motioned his children forward, then looked at Mary with an expression she couldn't decipher. She wished she knew what he was thinking, but his face was as hard to read as a partly cloudy sky that could bring rain or sun. After the agonizing wait for him to arrive, now that the big moment had finally come, she was just as unsure about her absurd plan as she had been the day she had made it.

Mary had made the choice to change her life forever just a few days earlier, right after she was laid off from Beiler's Quilt and Fabric Shop. She had loved working there. Loved the smell of new fabric and the whispery sound of scissors cutting cloth. Loved chatting with locals as they browsed bolts of fabric and dress patterns, or helping tourists choose one of the colorful, handmade quilts that sold on consignment. The shop had long been a staple in Bluebird Hills. Amish women knew it stocked everything they needed to clothe their families or sew a quilt. A steady stream of Lancaster County tourists sought it out for an "authentic" Amish experience.

At least until the discount franchise Sew-N-Save opened up across town. Tourists still came into Beiler's for the quilt selection, but most just snapped a few photos, gushed over the tiny, handsewn stitches, then left empty-handed once they saw the twelve-hundred-dollar price tag for a genuine, Amish-made quilt.

Mary's boss, Betty Beiler, had no choice but to let her go, even though Mary had worked at the shop for years. The pay had never been good, so Mary had no savings. And now, she couldn't make her mortgage payment. The Lancaster bank that specialized in financing Amish property had been threatening action if she didn't pay soon. She couldn't bear to lose her little bungalow. It was the home she had made for herself, even though she had no husband or children to share it with.

So it was no wonder that, as she sat alone in her living room, praying for a solution, an unusual notice in *The Budget* newspaper had caught her attention:

> Sugarcreek, Ohio: Silas Hochstetler is doing as well as can be expected after his house burned to the ground Wednesday night. He and his children escaped injury, but their home and the attached harness shop are a total loss. After much prayer, it wonders him if the best solution might be to marry. He needs a wife with a house and a place for his harness shop, and a willingness to mother his nine-year-old son and his sixteen-year-old daughter, who has been in a bit of trouble lately. In exchange, Silas would provide for all his wife's expenses. He has been a widower for nine years and hopes to find a sensible widow, agreeable to the ar-

rangement. His bishop and plenty of other folks in Sugarcreek will vouch for him.

Mary had read the letter several times, taken a long sip of tea and leaned back against the embroidered cushion in her armchair. She knew what she had to do.

Silas stood in the threshold of Mary's house, waiting for his children to catch up. He wouldn't go in without them. Mary hovered inside, looking fragile enough to blow away in the wind. She had a slight figure and features that were pale and even, but not memorable. She was neither pretty nor ugly, but somewhere in between. The hair tucked neatly beneath her *kapp* was an indistinct shade of brown. The *Englisch* would call her average. As an Amish woman, she was perfectly Plain. She could easily go unnoticed if someone passed her on the street.

And yet, something about her stood out

to Silas. Was it the flicker of courage combined with trepidation hiding behind her ordinary features? Was it the warmth in her dark gray eyes? Whatever it was, it brought beauty to her features that ran deeper than looks alone.

Maybe Silas was reading too much into the woman's face. But his instincts said he was right. He had always been good at sizing people up and her expression told a story that made his fingers twitch to reach out and take her hand.

"Daed." Silas's daughter, Becky, tugged at his sleeve. He felt his son's thin body press against his other side. He wrapped a protective arm around him, then pulled his attention from Mary to glance down at his daughter.

"Is that her?" she whispered.

"Ya."

"Then why are you just standing here?"

"I was waiting for you and your brother." But that wasn't the whole truth. His palms were sweating and his heart was knocking around in his chest. Suddenly, unexpectedly, he was too nervous to talk to the woman who would be his wife. All he could think was…*what will she think of me*?

He looked back up and watched Mary across the living room, waiting for them to enter. She looked down and smoothed the front of her blue cape dress before nervously looking back again. Her eyes darted from him to his children, then off into the distance, as if she were trying to figure out the least awkward way to speak to the stranger she would marry the next day.

"This is my son, Ethan, and my daughter, Becky," Silas said, breaking the silence as he shooed his children inside and pulled the door closed behind them, shutting out the howl of the wind with a gentle bang. The house felt warm and snug after the blustery journey through a January snowstorm.

"It's wonderful good to meet you all," Mary said with a bright, genuine smile that Silas felt all the way down to his toes.

They stared at one another for a moment.

Becky shifted her weight from one foot to the other and readjusted the battered suitcase clasped in her hands. The fire inside the woodstove crackled and glowed behind Mary, highlighting the softness of her features. She looked so lovely standing there, so shy and so obviously alone, that Silas felt a lump in his throat. For the first time in days—perhaps even months or years—he felt a surge of hope flood through him.

He had almost forgotten the feeling, especially after his house and business had been destroyed. It had seemed like a random, senseless accident, caused by a kerosene lantern and a gust of wind. That had been the last straw after the long, weary years of single fatherhood. But then, the letter postmarked Bluebird Hills, PA, had arrived, offering an unexpected new beginning.

He remembered clutching the paper in his hand as he had tried to visualize the woman who had written it. Was she kind? Was she committed to the faith? Was she someone he could sit beside on long, dark, winter evenings and talk to as a friend? Mary King had only included a few details about herself: she was hardworking, had always wanted children and was in need of just the sort of arrangement proposed in *The Budget*.

The whole community had rallied behind Silas after the fire. They would have helped him rebuild, but the bishop had recognized Silas's need to give his children a loving stepmother and a fresh start. Even so, the bishop had been skeptical as they stood at the site of Silas's ruined property, the smell of smoke lingering in the air above the charred timber where his house and harness shop once stood. He had taken the letter from Silas, looked over it, shaken his head and handed it back.

"You know, you could go about it in the normal way, ask a *gut* woman to walk out with you and all that," the bishop had said as he adjusted his black felt hat. "Drive her home from church services in your buggy, then propose after you get to know each other."

"You know I can't do that," Silas had said simply.

The bishop sighed. "It's been a long time since you lost your wife, Silas. Ethan was just a baby then. And none of that was your fault."

Silas's face had hardened as if a wall had come down. "It was. She was my wife. I should have been there for her. I should have found a way to save her from herself. I loved her, she trusted me, and I failed her." His jaw had tightened. "Never again."

"So you're proposing marriage with the intent to never love your new wife?"

"A marriage doesn't need love."

"I don't think you believe that."

"Of course, I do."

The bishop had rubbed his eyes. He had looked tired. "Then why bother to remarry?"

"The *kinner* need a mother. You know that. Especially Becky. I can't get through to her anymore. And I'd like to get her out of Sugarcreek, before she gets dragged into a wild *rumspringa*. After the *youngies* here went and got into all that trouble over in Millersburg last month, I can't trust her friends anymore. They've become a bad influence."

The bishop had nodded thoughtfully. "It's true that some of the *youngies* around here are taking their *rumspringa* too far. I know how hard that is after—"

"I don't want to talk about it. Just know that I won't let Becky end up like her mother."

"I know you won't. She's not going to leave the Amish. She's not going to make the choices Linda did. Linda was troubled, Silas. She was troubled long before she even met you."

"I told you, I don't want to talk about it." Silas had had to stop himself and take a deep breath. He had looked out over the snow-covered fields and pastures that stretched all the way to the horizon. "I'm sorry, Bishop. I didn't mean to speak that way to you."

"I know."

Silas had squeezed his eyes shut as he braced himself to talk about things that he never wanted to remember. He had taken another deep breath and opened his eyes. "After Linda left the faith and we lost her in the accident, I knew I had to do everything I could to protect the *kinner*. I can't let Becky go down the path her mother did. I'll do whatever it takes."

"You can only do so much. You have to trust *Gott* to keep Becky on the right path."

"Well, that's just it, ain't so? As Amish, we know that everything that happens to us is *Gott*'s will. So the fire that burned down my house and business had to have been planned by Him. Maybe it was to lead me in this new direction, to find a *gut* mother for my *kinner* and get Becky away from bad influences here. I never would have taken the risk to marry a stranger if I still had my home and livelihood."

The bishop had nodded slowly. “I can’t argue that. But I still don’t like the fact that you won’t consider a real marriage.”

“We’ve already discussed this. I won’t risk failing another woman. If we make this a business arrangement then we can keep our distance.” Silas had lowered his voice and his eyes. “She’ll be safer that way.”

“I think the heart you’re trying to protect is your own,” the bishop had said.

Silas had crossed his arms and studied the soft, black ash beneath his feet. “Do you support me or not?”

A long, awkward silence had followed. “*Ya*, Silas, I do,” the bishop had finally said. “But I’m sad for you and this woman you’re going to marry, whoever she is. I hope you can finally find a way to move on from your past after you leave Sugarcreek, for her sake if not for yours.”

Silas had wasted no time jotting down a quick reply to Mary King’s letter and posting it for next-day delivery. He had wanted to follow through right away, before he had second thoughts. In her letter, Mary had suggested that he use her barn for the harness shop. That would work just fine. The business would be up and running again just a few weeks from now. Becky and Ethan would have a mother and he would have someone to talk to. Silas had frowned at the thought. That was not what this arrangement would be about. He would have to stay on guard. It would be too easy to look to his new wife for comfort and companionship.

He knew how dangerous that could be.

Silas and his children had arrived in Bluebird Hills, Pennsylvania, three days later. Silas had been thankful that he had barely had time to think during the whirlwind move. Becky had been voicing more than enough concerns for the both of them. "It isn't the same as Holmes County," she had announced as they stepped out of the bus, drowsy and achy from the long ride.

"Nee," Silas had said. "It's Lancaster County."

Becky had made a face. "You know what I mean, *Daed*."

Ethan had stayed silent as he stepped closer to his father. He was shy and small for his age, but he had looked even smaller than usual as he pressed himself against Silas's side, eyes round as saucers as they took in the strange surroundings.

Silas had put an arm around Ethan as they surveyed the row of quaint little mom-and-pop shops lining Bluebird Hills's Main Street. Beyond the block of buildings were rolling hills of farmland blanketed by snow and dotted with red barns. A row of buggies stood in front of a coffee shop, a bookstore and a quilt shop, the horses waiting patiently in the frosty, January air. A handful of *Englisch* tourists wearing puffy jackets and thick scarves had hurried past with paper coffee cups clutched in their gloved hands.

"It looks like one of those *Englisch* postcards of Amish Country." Silas had given Becky a reassuring squeeze on the shoulder. She had felt too thin through her black winter cloak. "It seems nice."

Becky had not answered and when he had looked down at her face, her lip had been trembling. "It isn't home," she had said.

Even though he was nine years old, Ethan had slipped his small hand into Silas's. He had looked up at his father with big, questioning eyes.

Silas's chest had constricted. "*Nee*, but it will be."

"What if...?" A flicker of vulnerability had passed over Becky's features. "What if she doesn't like me, *Daed*?"

Silas's chest had tightened even more. "Is that what you're worried about?" He had wanted to reach down and scoop his daughter into his arms, the way he used to when she was little, and soothe away her fears. She still had the same blond hair from childhood, the same fair skin, flushed cheeks and the sprinkle of freckles across her nose. But she was not that child anymore, and she wouldn't accept his comfort.

After Silas's question, Becky's expression had changed and she had squared her shoulders. "*Nee.* I don't care what she thinks."

Silas had known better than to contradict her. It would only lead to another one of their arguments and he was too tired to deal with that after the long journey. He had just wished that he had some way to connect with her, to reassure her. He had started to put his arm around her shoulders, but she shrugged him away and stepped aside. Another little piece of Silas's heart had chipped away. "It's going to be *oll recht*, Becky. I promise."

"I know it is, *Daed*." But the expression on her face had said otherwise. She had crossed her arms against her father's words and the cold wind whipping down Main Street. "I don't want to talk about it."

"Oll recht," Silas had said, then headed toward the *Englisch* driver waiting for

them beside the bus stop, ready to whisk them to their new lives with a stranger.

Mary's heart was in her throat as her new family hovered just inside her house. She had been so busy worrying about what Silas thought of her that she had forgotten to worry about what he thought of his new home. Would the bungalow floor plan be spacious enough for him? Would the children like it? Was her barn alright for his harness shop? She swallowed hard as they stood in silence, the only sound the harsh whisper of the wind and the rumble of the fire in the woodstove. Silas had barely spoken since he arrived. Mary wondered if she had done something to upset him. Or perhaps he simply didn't like her. Would he still go through with the wedding now that he had seen his new fiancée and his new house?

Becky didn't speak to her at all. She just clutched her black cloak around her chest as if someone might take it from her.

Only Ethan seemed happy to see Mary, even though he clung to his father's arm as though he was afraid to let go. But he looked up at her and smiled. "Hello," he said. "You seem nice."

"Oh." Mary tried to think of the right thing to say. "I'm very glad you think so." She glanced to Silas, but his face remained stony. She could only hope that he agreed with his son. Another moment passed in awkward silence. "Well, here's the house," Mary said, then frowned when she thought about what an obvious statement that was. "I could show you around, if you like?" Anything would be better than staring at one another, unsure of what to say or do.

"I hope you like it. It's small, but it's cozy."

"It's smaller than I thought it would be," Becky said.

Mary felt embarrassed. "*Ya*. It's small, but cozy."

"You already said that."

Mary fiddled with the hem of her apron.

She couldn't look at Becky. "*Ya*. Well, it's true."

Silas sighed. "That's enough, Becky. Show some gratitude. The house is fine."

Fine. It wasn't exactly glowing praise, but Mary would take it as better than nothing. "Look around. It's all yours now." Her chest tightened as she said the words. Her little house had always been her sanctuary. Yes, it had been lonely there, but she had never had to share her space or compromise with anyone except her nephew, Gabriel, who had moved in after he graduated from the one room Amish schoolhouse. His father—Mary's brother—was harsh and judgmental, so Gabriel had been eager to get away from his childhood home. Mary understood how Gabriel felt. Her own father's criticism still echoed inside her head, years after he had passed away.

Gabriel had recently moved out of Mary's house to marry Eliza Zook, leaving Mary feeling more alone than ever. She had longed to fill her home with laughter again. But now she realized that the Hochstetlers were not as easy going as Gabriel. What if she couldn't get along with these strangers who were suddenly going to be family? Mary hadn't thought things through very well. She had been too desperate to find a solution to all her problems.

Mary watched as Silas surveyed the old, upholstered armchair, wooden rockers and braided-rag rug in the little room. Mary thought the knitted blankets and crocheted cushion covers made the space feel warm and homey, but she didn't know if Silas agreed. A calendar with a photograph of snowcapped mountains hung on the bare white wall and a tall, clunky propane lamp stood beside Mary's chair. Her worn Bible was lying open atop the scratched and dented end table. "*Ach*, I left my Bible out. Sorry, I didn't mean to leave a mess."

Silas gave her a strange look. "Never heard anyone apologize for reading their Bible before."

"I..." Mary wasn't sure how to explain. She just wanted everything to be perfect for her new family. She had been scrubbing and cleaning ever since she received Silas's reply to her letter, until the entire house smelled like Pine-Sol and lemon. "Let me show you the kitchen," Mary said. "Not that you'll be there much, Silas. Well, except it's eat-in, so the table's there. But Becky, you'll be baking with me, ain't so? We'll have a wonderful *gut* time, I'm certain sure. And Ethan, they'll be plenty of cookie dough for you." Mary stopped and shut her mouth. She was talking too much. It was her nerves. She just had so much to prove and she wanted so desperately for them all to be happy here, together.

Built in the 1940s, the kitchen had a retro feel. Mary hoped Silas wouldn't think it was too fancy. Except for taking out the electrical wiring, she hadn't changed much about the house since she bought it. There was a small, round dinette table in the corner, a propane-powered refrigerator, light green Formica countertops, a row of light green cabinets that matched the color of the beadboard walls, and an old-fashioned sink with exposed plumbing underneath. Mary had hung a green gingham curtain to hide the pipes and now she worried that Silas might think that was too fancy as well. She should have sewed a new curtain in a dark, solid fabric. "I'm sorry if it's too fancy." Mary picked at a crack in the countertop.

"It's a nice kitchen, Mary." Silas glanced around. "There's no decoration. Looks Plain to me."

"*Ya*, but that shade of green and the gingham and beadboard..." Mary cleared her throat and straightened up from the counter. "I'm glad you think it's *oll recht*."

Silas nodded.

"Your bedrooms are upstairs. They have sloped ceilings, so there's not a lot of space, especially for you, Silas."

"I'm sure they'll do just fine," Silas said

as he and Becky followed Mary out of the kitchen.

"My bedroom's in there." Mary nodded at a closed door off the living room as they filed past. The short staircase creaked as they walked up, and when Silas reached his room, the dimensions seemed to have shrunk. His head brushed the ceiling and his hands reached both walls when he extended his arms. Mary had scrubbed the floors twice on her hands and knees, washed the windows and laid out her very best quilt on the narrow bed. But now, all her efforts seemed in vain. The room simply wouldn't work. "This is the smallest room in the house. I thought the *kinner* needed the bigger one, since there's two of them. I'm sorry. I can switch with you. If you wouldn't mind moving my furniture up here, you can take my bedroom, where you could stand up straight. Or you could just use my furniture. That might be easier unless—"

"Mary..." Silas was frowning at her.

Mary bit her lip. She had said the wrong thing.

"I'm not taking your room. This is fine. I'll make do with the ceiling height."

"Oh. *Oll recht*. Well, if you change your mind…"

"I'm not going to change my mind. I'm not kicking you out of your own room."

Silas looked frustrated, which made Mary even more insecure. She turned to the children and forced a smile. "How would you like to see your room now? I fixed it up special, just for you."

Ethan nodded. Becky just shrugged.

"Thank Mary for fixing up a room for you, Becky."

"Danki," Becky said in a flat tone.

Mary had been saving their room for last, looking forward to the big reveal. She had spent hours getting it just right. But Becky didn't seem to care at all. "It's across from this one," Mary said. "But it's a little bigger. It'll be snug, but you'll both fit—"

"I have to share a room with Ethan?" Becky asked.

"I'm sorry—"

"You don't need to apologize, Mary," Silas said. "It's *gut* for *kinner* to live simply and learn to share."

His words bolstered her as she pushed the door open to reveal two single beds with metal frames. Each was neatly made with a star-of-Bethlehem quilt, one in shades of blue, the other in shades of pink. A faceless Amish doll sat atop the pink quilt and a teddy bear sat on the blue one. "I know you're both nearly grown," Mary said. "You're probably too old for dolls and stuffed animals, but I thought it looked nice…"

"It's a thoughtful touch," Silas said.

Ethan went straight to his bed and picked up the teddy bear. "I'm going to name him Teddy." His sweet, innocent manner sent a surge of warmth through her.

A row of pegs lined one wall, with two wooden chests underneath. A pink-and-blue braided-rag rug covered the worn hardwood floor. As a final touch, Mary had framed and hung an embroidery sampler on the wall that read God Bless This Home.

Mary held her breath as she waited for Becky's reaction. For the past two days, Mary had been secretly daydreaming that, as soon as her new daughter saw the room, she would turn to her, grin and rush into her arms, exclaiming how happy she was.

But Becky barely looked at the room before dropping onto the bed with a heavy sigh. The springs creaked beneath her weight.

"Do you...like it?" Mary asked.

"What, the room?" Becky sighed again, then shrugged. "It's okay, I guess."

Mary felt like she had been punched in the stomach. She knew it was silly to put so much expectation into Becky's reaction, but she had been so eager to make her happy. At least Ethan seemed content. He was still cuddling the teddy bear, even though most folks would say he was too old for it.

"It's a wonderful good room," Silas insisted. "You've put a lot of work into it."

Mary looked down. She turned away quickly, before she was tempted to pride, and headed out of the room. "I should put on some coffee. You've come a long way and you must be tired."

Silas trotted after her. Mary felt his hand on her shoulder when she reached the bottom of the staircase. "Mary."

"Ya?"

"You don't have to do all of this for us. The rooms are great, but..."

Mary spun around and saw that he was frowning. She couldn't figure out why.

"I just want to make Ethan and Becky happy." Mary hesitated. "I just want to make *you* happy. I've never been married before. I..." She tightened her grip on the banister. She had already said too much. She waited for Silas's response, but he just looked at her through weary eyes, as though he felt too tired and defeated by life to tell her what he was thinking. His jaw tightened and Mary wondered if she had upset him somehow, but then he responded in a soft, sad voice, "*Danki*, Mary. It was very thoughtful of you. I just don't think..." Then he cut himself off, shook his head and managed a slight smile. "We'll talk about everything later. You've been very welcoming. I appreciate that."

Mary felt a wave of hope rise through her to form a lump in her throat. He appreciated her, or he appreciated what she had done for him, at least. It was a good start. As he looked into her eyes, she sensed there was so much more that Silas wanted to say but couldn't. He seemed so distant, yet kind, which confused her. She wanted to press him to tell her what he was going to say, but she didn't want to cause any conflict. They had only just met, after all.

"We should get the *kinner* settled," Silas said. Mary recognized that he was trying to change the subject to avoid telling her what he was thinking. "And your bishop's expecting us, ain't so?"

"Oh." Mary's face fell. "I'm sorry, Silas. I'm afraid I've already made a mess of things." Her eyes watered and, for a moment, Mary was afraid that she might cry. But then, her expression hardened. She cleared her throat and smoothed the front of her crisp, white apron. "I haven't told the bishop you're coming." She looked past him, out the window, to watch the snowflakes drifting from a white sky. She had failed at this important task, like so many things in life. "I'm sorry. I know I was supposed to tell him. But I..."

"You couldn't make yourself do it."

Mary's eyes shot up to meet his. "*Ya*. I kept putting it off, until—" she gave a sheepish little smile "—it was too late and here we are." Her father always used to say that she was a disappointment. Now, years later, Mary still froze when she had to do something that might bring disapproval.

She had learned to avoid confrontation and reshape her personality to fit others' expectations. Mary had gotten that from her late mother. She had made herself smaller and smaller trying to please Mary's father. Mary believed that her mother had died of a broken heart that had eventually collapsed under the pressure to be good enough.

"Are you afraid that he'll stop the wedding?" An expression crossed Silas's face that could have been frustration or sympathy. Mary couldn't tell which.

"*Nee*. He'll be understanding. He's a *gut* bishop. But that's what makes it so hard, ain't so? I couldn't… I didn't want to disappoint him." She blinked, then her words hit her and she flinched. "I don't mean that *you'll* disappoint him! You seem like a very nice man. It's just that, well, I mean that—"

"It's *oll recht*." Silas reached out and put a big, calloused hand on her arm. "I understand."

Warmth surged through Mary from the gentle touch. If she could just let go and trust him… She had never experienced that security before. But it was too soon to let down her guard. She needed to stay strong.

"What we're doing is unusual," Silas continued. His eyes remained on hers, steady and reassuring. "Folks might talk. They might even say we shouldn't go through with it."

"*Ya*. They might. And I don't want to let them down."

Silas stared at her, as if trying to figure her out. "I don't think you could do that if you tried."

Mary let out a little laugh and looked away. "You don't know me yet."

Silas paused. Mary felt him studying her. "Let's go meet that bishop of yours. I'll help you face it."

Mary swallowed hard and met his gaze. "You will?"

"For certain sure. We're going to be married, aren't we? I figure this is my problem as much as yours."

Mary wondered what he meant by that. Was he supporting her, or was he frustrated by the trouble she was already causing him? She hoped with all her heart that he wasn't put off by her cowardice.

Mary's buggy horse, Red Rover, trotted along Bluebird Hills's snowy back roads as they headed toward the bishop's house. A few flurries blew across the damp, gray sky, but the storm had lifted and the plows had cleared most of the pavement. The horse's heavy hoofbeats punctuated the silence that hung in the cold air and settled across the bench seat. Ethan huddled between them, taking in the new surroundings without speaking. Mary ached to put an arm around his thin shoulders. Becky sat in the back, her mouth clamped in a tight line as she hugged herself for warmth. Miles of countryside spread out beyond them, the brown and green fields dusted white, as if sprinkled with powdered sugar.

"You could have driven the buggy, you know," Silas said as he adjusted the reins. "It's yours, after all. I sold mine before leaving Sugarcreek." Mary wondered if Silas was criticizing her for suggesting that he drive. No, she decided. He was trying to be nice.

"It will be yours soon," Mary said.

Silas nodded, keeping his eyes on the road ahead. "True enough."

What Mary didn't say was that she liked that Silas was driving. It was nice to sit back and watch the fields and pastures roll by as snowflakes drifted down like feathers to tickle her nose and cover the farmland. She liked feeling taken care of by a man who wanted to marry her.

Well, maybe he didn't exactly want to marry *her*, specifically. He didn't know her yet. But he wanted to marry the *idea* of her. And that was enough. It had to be.

"It's here." Mary pointed toward a tidy

farm in the distance. "The house up on the hill, behind the pond and the split-rail fence."

Silas tugged the reins to guide Red Rover into the driveway. Gravel crunched beneath the buggy wheels as the horse strained to pull them uphill. He whinnied and broke into a gallop that pressed Mary against the back of the bench seat.

"Easy now, big fella," Silas murmured as he tugged hard at the reins. Red Rover snorted and shook his head, then steadied his pace. "You *oll recht*?" Silas asked with a quick glance at Mary.

She beamed inside. No one had asked her that kind, simple question in so long. Especially not a man. She wanted Silas to put his hand in hers to reassure her, but that was out of the question, of course. "*Danki*, I'm fine. Red Rover can go too fast sometimes. He has a mind of his own. I'm sorry he's not always easy to drive." Mary felt a stab of guilt. She wished she had a better horse to offer. She had grown to love Red Rover, but he was a difficult animal. She had bought him cheap, at an auction for retired racehorses that no one wanted. She had learned right away why he had been such a bargain.

"It's not your fault that he wants to run. By the look of him, it's in his blood. You don't need to apologize."

Mary didn't know what to say to that, so she just looked away. She was used to everything being her fault. That's what her father and older brother had always said to her. Now, she barely spoke to her brother, even though he had stayed in Lancaster County after their other siblings had scattered to other Amish communities as soon as they were old enough to get away.

"Whoa," Silas said as he pulled the reins. Red Rover shook his head and danced sideways before skidding to a stop. "Time to tell the bishop our *lecherich* plan." He flashed a lopsided grin at Mary that made her heart do a little flip-flop in her chest.

"And you like to say that *I'm* ridiculous,

Daed," Becky said from the back of the buggy. "Just because I'm a *youngie*. But I'm not the one running off to marry a stranger."

Mary didn't turn around to see Becky's expression. She hoped the girl was joking, but was too afraid to check. Was Silas's daughter against this plan? The thought was too worrying to consider. Mary had imagined that Becky would be the daughter she had always wanted. They would bake and sew together, and talk about boys and youth group. That connection would help make up for all the years that Mary had missed, when she had longed to be a mother, but lived alone in her little bungalow.

Silas jumped from his seat and jogged around to Mary's side of the buggy before she had a chance to open her door. She tried to hide her smile as he helped her to the ground. His thoughtfulness warmed her as she faced the cold air...and the reprimand she knew was coming.

Edna Yoder, the bishop's plump, gray-haired wife, opened the farmhouse door when Silas knocked. She stared at the four of them in surprise as they huddled on the porch, blowing their hands and stomping their feet against the dropping temperature.

"*Kumme* in," Edna said after the moment of surprise passed. She gave Mary a quick hug before turning to Silas and his children. "You must be new to Bluebird Hills."

"*Ya*, we are. I'm Silas Hochstetler. This is my *dochder*, Becky and my *sohn*, Ethan. We're here to speak to your husband."

Edna gave Mary a concerned glance. "Is everything *oll recht*?"

"I hope so," Mary said quietly. Her stomach was already dropping to her feet and she hadn't even seen Bishop Amos yet.

Edna studied Silas for a moment before waving them all into the parlor and leaving to fetch Amos from the barn. A black, potbellied stove filled the small room with heat and the scent of woodsmoke. Edna's quilts lay folded on the back of the couch and on a quilt rack beside a rocking chair. Mary had been in this snug little living room too often to count, but this was the first time she had ever felt dread. She couldn't bear to disappoint the bishop.

"*Kumme*, sit by me," Silas said to Mary. The invitation gave her strength. She felt like they were already becoming a team, even though they were still strangers. Ethan clung to his father and wedged between them, while Becky hung back, alone. "You seem like a very *gut bu*," Mary whispered to Ethan. "I'm glad you're here."

Ethan's big, brown eyes gazed up at her with shy adoration. She knew, in that moment, that she was doing the right thing. She scooted closer to him and he leaned his head on her shoulder. "He's exhausted," she murmured to Silas.

"It was a long journey here," Silas said. His expression softened for the first time since Mary had met him as he watched her with his son.

They heard the front door open and close, and the stomping of snowy boots on a doormat, then Amos burst into the room without the usual twinkle in his eye. "Something is wrong?"

Ethan's head popped up from Mary's shoulder and he looked at his father with alarm.

"Ach, nee." Mary glanced from Silas to Amos. "Well, not exactly." She opened her mouth to explain but no words came out.

Silas stood up. "We're getting married."

He had said it for her. Relief flooded Mary, although her cheeks still burned with embarrassment.

A look of surprise flashed across Amos's face. "Mary, who is this man?"

Edna stepped forward from where she hovered in the doorway and motioned toward Ethan and Becky. "Why don't you *kumme* with me and let your *daed* talk to the bishop. Becky, you can help me with the cake I'm baking."

Becky looked at Silas and he nodded.

She heaved a dramatic sigh. “Fine. I miss out on everything.”

Ethan didn’t move.

“It’s *oll recht, sohn*,” Silas said in a low voice. “I’ll be right here.”

“There’s some cake batter in it for you,” Edna said.

“Go on, *sohn*.” Silas gave an encouraging nudge and Ethan slid off the couch to follow the bishop’s wife. He glanced back at them from the doorway with a look that made Mary want to throw her arms around him and hug the anxiety away. Becky trailed after Edna and Ethan, her shoulders hunched over and her arms crossed against her chest.

They waited until they heard the kitchen door close before speaking again. “Mary?” Amos prompted. He was a small man with wizened features and a shiny head that was almost completely bald.

“This is Silas, my…fiancé.”

“Your fiancé? Then why have I never seen him before?”

"Because we've never met until this afternoon."

Amos stared for a moment. Then he shook his head and sank into the wooden rocking chair opposite Mary and Silas. "I think you'd better explain."

Silas recapped the events that had led him to Bluebird Hills, then shrugged. "And here I am."

Amos let out a sharp whistle. "Just like that."

"Just like that," Silas said.

Amos turned to Mary. "You don't feel forced into this, do you? Is there a problem here that I don't know about?"

A thousand thoughts raced through Mary's mind. The lonely evenings spent in silence by her woodstove, the longing for a child, the sharp ache she felt whenever she walked into a home bustling with noise and life. And, of course, there was the need for Silas's income. Now was her chance to tell the bishop she needed help to keep her house from foreclosure. He would make sure the community organized a charity mud sale, like they had done to save the Millers's farm and gift shop.

Mary's pulse thudded in her throat. She looked at Silas. His warm, brown eyes, steady and reassuring, held hers. Footsteps thumped softly from across the house, followed by laughter. Mary wanted to be in the kitchen with Becky and Ethan, baking for her family and laughing together. If Mary told Amos her financial trouble, she would lose her chance at having children and a husband. Silas, Ethan and Becky would go back to Holmes County and she would stay here, alone.

"It's my decision," Mary said. "I want to do this."

"Why, Mary? You've always been sensible. You've never done anything to set yourself apart."

Mary's brow crinkled. "Bishop Amos, can't you see I'm doing this to be like everyone else, *not* to set myself apart?"

Amos's expression shifted. "*Ach*, Mary. I think I understand now." He looked at her with sympathetic eyes before turning to Silas. "Mary is a *gut* woman. I've known her for many years. It's my job as bishop of this community to look out for her. How can I trust you to be a *gut* husband to her?"

"That's a reasonable question, Bishop. I've brought letters vouching for my character from my bishop in Sugarcreek and all the elders of the church district. They have concerns, same as you, about this arrangement, but they all support me. They know I'll provide for Mary."

Amos studied Silas for a moment. "Providing for a *fraa* isn't all that marriage is about. What about her heart?"

"I don't want to be alone anymore," Mary interrupted. She wouldn't put Silas on the spot by making him answer that question. She didn't expect him to fall in love with her. That wasn't part of the agreement.

"Some of the loneliest people I've met are married," Amos said. "Especially when their husbands think providing for their family is all that marriage requires of them."

Silas shifted in his seat.

"A woman needs love and friendship from her husband, same as a husband needs love and friendship from his wife."

"Amos, it's *oll recht*," Mary said. "It's a *gut* enough arrangement, even if it's not a perfect one."

The bishop shook his head. "Don't sell yourself short, Mary."

"I'm thirty-four years old, Amos. I don't think I'm selling myself short."

"*Ach*, Mary. I wish you could see yourself for who you are. And I wish you had told me about this. Why did you keep it a secret? I can't help you when you hide things from me."

Mary looked down. "I'm sorry, Amos. I was too embarrassed. This isn't the way we do things."

"*Nee*, it's not." Amos sighed and ran his fingers through his long white beard. "But there's nothing against it in the *Ordnung*."

Mary raised her gaze to him. "Then you won't stop the marriage?"

"*Nee*. But make very sure of your decision, Mary. You know that we don't allow divorce. Amish marriages are for life. Once you say your vows, there's no going back."

Mary had been on her own since her ex-fiancé jilted her fourteen years ago for a woman from Bird-in-Hand who baked a perfect pie crust and could make everyone laugh. Mary wasn't funny or entertaining. She was quiet and unassuming. She didn't know how to make anyone love her, even though it was all she had ever wanted.

No one else had asked to court her. No one had wanted to share a life with her. Financial instability had driven her to make this decision, but even if she could afford her mortgage, she still had reason to go ahead with the arranged marriage.

Mary drew up her chin and took a deep breath. This was her chance to have a family of her own, and she would take it. She had always chosen the safe path. Now she would take the greatest risk of her life and she would not look back.

Chapter Two

Silas stood in the Millers's farmyard, watching the crowd of people clustered around the gray buggies parked in the trampled grass. Women in pink, purple, blue, and green cape dresses held babies on their hips and chatted as their husbands unhitched their horses. Children scampered past the chicken coops and dodged icy mud puddles until their parents reminded them to mind their church manners.

Silas's two children waited by his side, tense and silent as they took in the scene around them. They were surrounded by strangers, except for Amos and Edna, who had invited them to stay over the night before. But Amos had slipped inside to prepare for the service and Edna was chatting with another family. Silas was not used to being alone in a crowd. He had known everyone in his church district back home.

"Where's Mary?" Ethan asked in a small voice.

"I don't see her," Silas said as he scanned the gathering. "She might not be here yet."

Ethan looked up at his father's face with hopeful eyes. "We're going home with her after the service, ain't so?"

"Ya."

"And we won't ever have to leave?" Ethan asked.

"Nee," Silas said. He wished he felt as certain as he sounded. What if Mary didn't show up? What if she backed out of their arrangement? He wouldn't be surprised. Silas knew that he must have seemed hard and unapproachable when they met the day before. His heart was still soft, some-

where deep inside, but he was too afraid to let Mary know that. His late wife had known, and she had taken advantage of his need for love.

Silas's mind churned with worry but, deep down, he wanted to go ahead with the wedding. Mary seemed kind and considerate. And he could tell that there was a lively intelligence hiding behind her quiet demeanor. He would like a chance to draw that out of her, to encourage and reassure her.

Silas sighed. No. He had to remember to be careful and keep his distance. There was too much at stake. Too much to protect them both from.

Silas saw Becky give a small, shy wave out of the corner of his eye. He followed her gaze to a group of *youngies*. There were several boys who looked to be around Becky's age and all of them were smiling at her. Silas glanced back at Becky. She was smiling in return, her cheeks flushed red, and her eyes full of sparkle that hadn't been there a minute ago.

Silas's chest constricted. He had brought Becky here to get her away from a bad group of *youngies*. Well, that wasn't the only reason, but it sure had made the decision easier. His job was to protect his daughter and he would make sure he did, no matter what. She was precious and vulnerable and he would never let any harm befall her.

Especially if that harm came in the form of a handsome, charming young man, ready to sweep her off her feet. Silas knew how easy it was to fall for the wrong person. He had fallen head over heels for Becky's mother and that relationship had nearly destroyed him. It had been worth it to have Becky and Ethan, but Silas wanted to spare Becky from ever suffering the way he had. He wanted to make sure she chose a good husband who would love and support her and encourage her to stay in the faith.

How could he know if any of those boys watching her from across the farmyard were good or bad for her? The safest thing was to keep them all away from her for as long as he could. When she was a few years older, she would be able to make better, wiser choices than she would now.

"We should head inside," Silas said. Becky didn't respond and she didn't take her eyes off the group of boys.

"Come on—"

A man stepped in front of Silas before he could finish his sentence. He was tall and heavy set, with a thick jaw and what looked like a permanent scowl.

"These your *kinner*?" the man asked.

"Ya," Silas said. He didn't like the man's tone and he instinctively stepped closer, putting himself between the stranger and his children.

"Uh huh." The man rubbed his chin. "I figure you must be the man who's come here to marry my sister. You're the only fellow here who's got two kids with him and no *fraa* around. Plus, you and the *kinner* don't look like you belong here. Your girl's dress is too bright for this district's *Ordnung*." He narrowed his eyes. "And the cuff on her sleeves looks too wide. Best get that fixed."

This was Mary's brother? Silas wasn't sure how to respond for a moment. He had never seen two siblings who appeared to be such polar opposites of each other.

"Oh!" Edna hurried over from where she had been gushing over a newborn baby in a young mother's arms. "I didn't think you'd make it, Elmo."

"You mean you didn't think I'd bother to show up."

Edna flinched.

"Got your message at my phone shanty late last night. Could have let me know sooner."

"We just found out yesterday that Mary planned to get married today," Edna said. "And it seemed like the right thing to let you know about it, in case you wanted to *kumme* support her."

Elmo grunted. "*Vell*, I guess she's got to get married fast because she knows it's her last chance. No one else wants to marry her." Elmo chuckled and looked at Silas. "You sure you want to?"

Silas felt hot inside. How dare this man—Mary's own brother—speak like this about her? "I think you've said enough," Silas said quietly, as he stared Elmo down. He was careful to keep his tone steady and calm.

Elmo laughed and slapped Silas on the back. "Just a joke between men, that's all." He shook his head. "Still, it is hard to believe someone's finally going to marry Mousy Mary."

Edna sucked in her breath. "Elmo, can you please try and be more supportive?"

Elmo shrugged. "I'm only telling the truth." He glanced around the farmyard. "Where is Mary, anyway?"

"I'm sure she'll be here soon," Edna said.

"Or is she too scared to show up?" Elmo asked. "That sounds like her."

"Elmo, did you *kumme* to support your *schwester* or to criticize her?" Edna asked.

Elmo lifted his hands in a gesture of innocence. "I'm here to support her, of course. Isn't it obvious?"

"*Nee*, it is not," Silas said.

"Ah, look," Elmo said. "There she is."

They all turned to watch Mary's buggy pull into the driveway. "Time to go congratulate my *schwester*." Elmo walked away quickly, taking long strides across the grass as he adjusted his black felt hat.

Edna let out a long breath. "I'm afraid I made a mistake telling him about the wedding. But Elmo is the only family that Mary has around here besides Elmo's *sohn*, Gabriel. It seemed like the right thing to do." Edna shook her head. "I should have waited until I could discuss it with Mary this morning, but I knew it would have been too late by then. You see, I didn't think about it until after she had left our house last night."

Silas knew that well-meaning people like Edna thought that it was always best to include family. He had learned the hard way that that simply wasn't always the case. His late wife would have caused a scene too.

"It will be okay," Silas said as he watched Elmo approach Mary's buggy. It would be okay because Silas would make sure that it was. He gave a quick nod to Edna and set off across the farmyard, his jaw set and his eyes hard.

Silas could see that Mary and Elmo were engaged in conversation, but he couldn't make out the words. Elmo stood with his back to Silas, his elbow against the buggy's doorframe, as he leaned into Mary. Silas picked up his pace. He wanted to be there for his bride. Maybe he was overstepping, but it felt right to stand up for her.

As Silas neared them, Elmo shook his head, turned from the buggy, and walked away. Silas could hear him whistling, so he thought that everything must be alright.

But when Silas reached Mary, he could see tears sparkling in her eyes. She wiped them away quickly, straightened in her seat, and forced a smile. "Oh, hello, Silas."

"Hi, Mary. You okay?"

"Ya."

Silas raised his eyebrows. "You sure about that? I, uh, just met your *bruder*."

Mary stiffened, but managed to keep the smile on her face. She waved her hand. "*Ach*, it's nothing. You know how brothers can be."

Silas knew that Mary was making excuses, but he didn't want to embarrass her, so he just nodded, then glanced to the row of parked buggies, where Elmo was unhitching a horse. "He's not going to stay for the ceremony?"

"Um, *nee*. He just came to... *Vell*, I don't know why he came. To meet you, I guess."

Silas knew there was more to the story than Mary wanted to tell. But now it made more sense why she seemed so timid and unsure of herself. The rest of her family had probably been a lot like her brother—

where else would Elmo have learned to be like that? She had probably been criticized her whole life.

As Silas looked down at Mary, all he wanted to do was scoop her up, hold her, and tell her that he would keep her safe now. She was so strong and brave to push back the tears and try to go on. But he could see how hurt she was. He started to tell her that he wanted to protect her, that he *would* protect her.

But he didn't know how to explain how he felt. And he didn't know how to wipe away years of hurt. Besides, he was a stranger to her. She might not even want his help. So he sighed, stepped back, and gave a polite nod. "I'll see to your horse." It was the best he could do to show her that he cared.

Mary asked Silas to go inside with his children, without her. She needed a minute to compose herself, but didn't admit that to him. She just said she needed to speak to a friend first. It was a good enough excuse.

The crowd in the farmyard was thinning out, but her friend, Arleta Kauffman, had just pulled in. She was running late, which was perfect timing under the circumstances. While Arleta parked, Mary hid from the congregation in her own buggy, blotting her face with her sleeve to hide her tears.

When Mary had first caught sight of Elmo in the farmyard, she had felt a small spark of hope that he wanted to support her, maybe even to stand and say a blessing during the ceremony. She should have known better. Elmo was not going to change, no matter how much she wanted him to, no matter how many times she forgave him.

Elmo had only paid a visit out of curiously, apparently. And to enjoy a good laugh at her expense for jumping into an arranged marriage. Then he had left to get back to his own church district in time to attend his own service. She doubted that she would see him again for another few years. He usually didn't bother to visit her.

Thankfully, Silas didn't appear to be

anything like her brother. Instead, he had seemed protective of her. But perhaps she was just imagining that because she wanted it to be true. He might even agree with what Elmo thought about her. Her heart longed to be loved, but she knew that she could not always have what she wanted, even if that longing tore her apart inside.

Mary exhaled and looked out at the familiar faces in the farmyard that she had known since childhood. None of them knew about her plan—not even Arleta, the only other woman Mary knew in Bluebird Hills who was still unmarried and in her midthirties.

How could Mary stand in front of them today and announce that she would be married to a stranger? She had spent a restless night staring into the darkness from beneath her sixteen-patch quilt, until she had given up and lit the kerosene lantern. She had tried rereading old copies of *The Budget* to soothe herself to sleep, but every time she came to a wedding announcement, the reminder jolted her wide-awake.

"Why are you still sitting in your buggy?"

Mary jumped, then turned to see Arleta by her elbow. Her face looked pinched and thin, as it always did. Arleta had spent months shut up in her house after she was injured in a buggy accident. But after taking time to heal and working hard at rehabilitation, she was beginning to get her old life back again.

Arleta looked at Mary with her dark eyes. "You're sitting there staring like you're sleepwalking. *Kumme*, get inside before you catch cold. It's freezing out here."

Mary bit her lip as she slid out of her buggy. "I've got to tell you something, Arleta. I should have told you sooner, but I was afraid you wouldn't approve."

"Well, can you wait to tell me until we get inside? Whatever it is, I'm sure it's *oll recht*. You never do anything outside of the ordinary. Steady and reliable, that's you, Mary."

"You mean boring?"

Arleta laughed. "Boring isn't a bad thing, Mary. I like boring. Not that you're boring. Because you're not."

Arleta was backtracking now, but it was clear what she thought about Mary. Would Silas find her boring too? Had all the potential suitors who had passed her over thought she was boring? At least Arleta had called her reliable. That was a good thing. But it wasn't a quality that grabbed a man's attention. Mary had never grabbed any man's attention. She had always assumed that she was too average-looking for that. And too boring, apparently. She sighed. "Arleta, I don't know whether you're making me feel better or worse."

"*Ach*, well, you're making me feel cold." Arleta tugged at Mary's arm. "*Kumme* on. Let's get in there before I get one of my headaches."

Arleta's nine-year-old twin nephews

zipped by, elbowing one another and shouting. "Slow down, Ned and Newt!" Arleta called after them. "Get inside the house. The service is about to start."

Mary followed Arleta up the steps of the farmhouse's wraparound porch. They passed the row of empty rocking chairs and pulled open the front door. Ned and Newt shoved past them, into the cozy warmth of the entry hall. "Watch it, boys. And say excuse me," Arleta cautioned.

"Excuse me!" both boys shouted in unison as they hurried to find their friends before the long service began.

Mary and Arleta hung their black winter bonnets and cloaks on the pegs on the wall, then adjusted the *kapps* they wore. The soft murmur of voices filled the entry hall, along with a billow of hot air from the woodstove and propane heaters in the adjacent rooms. Mary rubbed her red, chapped hands together to stop the tingling from the sudden change in temperature.

"Now," Arleta said as they made their way into a spacious living room. "What was it you wanted to tell me?" Mary hesitated as she stared at the women and men seated on the long rows of backless benches. Like most of the Amish houses in Bluebird Hills, the Millers's living room was extralong to accommodate all the portable benches for church services. To make space, the men had pushed aside a battered blue couch, a rocking chair and a wooden crate filled with old copies of *The Budget*. A stack of fresh-cut kindling was lying on the brick hearth, beside a roaring fire.

But Mary wasn't paying attention to the room. Her eyes had gone straight to Silas Hochstetler, who sat on a bench with Ethan close beside him, while the other men chatted and took their seats nearby. Silas looked strong and determined and Mary's breath faltered at the reminder that this was real. She would be a married woman by dinnertime. Becky sat beside Edna on the women's side of the room, her arms crossed and her head down. Mary wanted to give her the hug she obviously needed.

Arleta noticed Silas right away, despite the commotion as the crowd jostled to find their places along the rows of benches. "Who's that?"

Mary cleared her throat. "Who?"

"The *gut*-looking stranger right there. He's sitting with the pale, frail-looking boy." Arleta's eyes cut to her friend. "You know exactly who that is, don't you? You can't keep a secret. It shows all over your face." Arleta's eyes narrowed as she stared at Mary. "Does he have something to do with whatever it is you didn't tell me outside? What exactly have you been keeping from me, Mary?"

"*Ach*, Arleta." Mary shook her head. "It's too late now." She felt like everyone in the room was whispering about Silas…and maybe about her, too. "I can't back out." *And I don't think I want to*, she thought. But she didn't admit that to Arleta.

"Back out of what?" Arleta asked slowly.

Silas turned his head and caught sight of Mary. He gave a solemn, reassuring nod from across the room that sent a warm wave rippling through her. Mary nodded back and smiled.

"Mary, I saw that look he gave you. And the one you gave him back. There's something going on between you two. I know it."

Mary shook her head. "There's nothing going on. I mean, there is, but not like that. I've only met him once."

"That's quite a look for a stranger to give."

"He's not exactly a stranger."

"Well, do you know him or not?"

"It's complicated."

Arleta rolled her eyes. "No, it's not. It's a simple question."

"If only that were true, Arleta."

Arleta studied Mary for a moment. "You can't mean…" Arleta blinked rapidly.

"What?" Mary asked.

"Ha! Now I know what you meant when you said you can't back out now. Especially since Edna brought a big bowl of creamed celery for after the service today. Creamed celery can only mean one thing."

"Not necessarily," Mary said. "People don't just eat celery at a wedding."

"Nice try," Arleta said. "It seems you have a lot of explaining to do."

"I know," Mary said.

"Do you love him?" Arleta asked.

"I don't even know him."

"Oh, Mary, what have you done?"

Mary didn't have time to answer. And, anyway, how could she when she was asking herself the same question? The bishop had taken his place at the center of the crowd and was raising his hands for silence. Mary hurried to an empty seat on the nearest bench and Arleta followed close behind. *Tell me*, she mouthed as they sat down.

I will, Mary mouthed back. But not now. It was all she could do to keep from passing out in the stuffy, crowded room. Had services always been this claustrophobic? No, because she had never felt this way before. Black spots threatened the edge of her vision as her heart pounded. The room began to shift in front of her. She needed to jump up and run as fast as she could, as far away as possible. Her entire body was shouting to escape. Arleta moved a steady hand to Mary's knee and held it there. "It's *oll recht*," she whispered. "I don't know what's going on with this *lecherich* wedding, but I do know you're having an anxiety attack. I have them, too. Take a deep breath and let it out slowly. I'm right here beside you. Whatever's happening, it will be *oll recht*. I promise. Just breathe."

Mary spent the rest of the service focusing on her breath. In and out. Slow and steady. Arleta kept a hand on her the entire time. Mary felt better knowing she had a friend who supported her, no matter how outrageous her plan might be. But that didn't change the fact that she was about to commit her life to a complete stranger.

Toward the end of the three-hour service, after the last hymn had been sung and Bishop Amos had finished preaching the second sermon, it was finally time. He stepped forward and looked at Mary. "We've got an unexpected addition to the service today," he announced.

People turned to glance at one another.

"Mary and Silas, *kumme* forward, please."

Arleta squeezed Mary's knee and gave her a firm nod. "Go on," she whispered. Mary stumbled up in a daze. She felt every eye on her as she made her way to the front of the congregation. Courting couples usually kept their marriage plans a secret until a month or so before the ceremony, but this was something else entirely.

"You all know Mary King," Amos said. "Silas Hochstetler and his *kinner* come to us from Holmes County. Silas and Mary are getting married today."

A wave of gasps and whispers erupted from the rows of benches.

Amos held up a hand. "I know this is a surprise." He shot Mary a look that made her stomach drop to her feet. She wanted to follow it and sink right into the floor. "But I've decided to bless the union. They both have *gut* reason for making this decision, hasty as it is. It isn't our usual way of doing things, for sure and certain, to tack on a wedding to the end of a service like this, especially without announcing it a few weeks in advance. But Silas needs to move his business into Mary's barn right away, so they don't have time to wait."

The room blurred around Mary as she tried to shut out the whispers and murmurs. All she could do was stare at Silas and hold on until this was over. His warm brown eyes caught hers and held her gaze.

"It's *oll recht*," he whispered. "We're in this together."

That was all that Mary needed to hear. Suddenly the floor felt steady beneath her feet and her breathing came easily.

She wasn't alone anymore.

Chapter Three

Silas knew he had said the wrong thing. Mary's face had changed as soon as the words were out of his mouth. He had wanted to comfort her, but that had been a mistake, because now she stared up at him with hope in her eyes, as if he was a hero come to rescue her.

He was no hero.

Silas tried to harden his expression, but it was too late. Mary believed in him now. She was expecting a friend and perhaps even more, someday. But Silas knew he could give her none of that.

Silas felt much older than his thirty-six

years as he listened to Amos read the traditional marriage verses from the Bible. He felt everyone's attention on him; including Mary, the bishop, the entire congregation, Ethan, who watched wide-eyed, and Becky, who slouched on the wooden bench and stared at him with a heart-wrenching mix of hope and fear. The pressure to live up to it all was unbearable. How could he ever be the husband and father they expected? He felt woozy. But he had to tamp down all those fears and frustrations. He had to show everyone that he was confident and in control. That was how a man was supposed to be, wasn't it?

"Silas?" Amos was frowning at him.

"Sorry, what?"

"Say 'I do.'"

"*Ach*, right. Of course. I do."

A small, soft exhale of relief escaped Mary's lips. She must have been afraid that he was going to back out and shame her in front of the entire church district. She looked so vulnerable, standing there in her starched white *kapp* and freshly ironed, pink dress. He should tell her that he was happy to marry her, that he saw her intelligence and kindness, and that he could see himself falling in love with her eventually.

But he clamped his mouth shut instead. He remembered another day like this one, when he had married another woman who had looked up at him with the same hope and expectation in her eyes. Linda had been madly in love with him, and he had been madly in love with her. It had been a wild, rocky courtship, with wonderful highs and terrible lows. Silas had believed that once they married, Linda would settle down and find peace.

She had not.

Instead, she had grown more troubled. And the more he had reached out to her, the more self-destructive she had become. She had begun to drink and, after Ethan was born, to disappear for long stretches at a time, until one day, she stopped coming home at all. Linda had jumped the fence and abandoned the Amish faith, leaving him and their children alone to deal with the aftermath of the storm she had created.

The worst part was that he could never feel angry at her. Not when she had been in so much pain. Silas had sensed that she was running from something inside herself, something bigger than he could protect her from. But that didn't take away the guilt.

Then, there had been that terrible day when the *Englisch* police had knocked on his door, hats in their hands… Silas shoved away the memories. He would do everything he could to make it right this time—which meant keeping as much distance as possible from his new wife. He wouldn't risk failing Mary. She was too good for him, too innocent and hopeful. The best thing for her was to keep this marriage strictly business.

"Go forth in *Gott*'s name," Amos said, jerking Silas back to the moment. It was over. Silas and Mary were officially husband and wife.

The next hour passed in a blur as everyone in the church district took a turn to introduce themselves and welcome Silas and his children to Bluebird Hills. Most of them had traditional Lancaster County names: Miller, Zook, King, Yoder, Beiler. It was a lot to keep straight and soon all the friendly faces ran together. Ethan clung to his side, even when two identical twin boys with auburn hair and freckles asked him to play marbles with them. Ethan just shook his head without saying a word. Becky stood behind them, twisting her hands and cutting her eyes to the door. His children had always been anxious, like their mother, and Silas wished he could take them to Mary's house—their house—where they could be alone to adjust.

Instead, he made his way through the buffet line, where the women piled creamed celery, cold ham, fresh-baked bread with peanut-butter church spread, brown-butter mashed potatoes, fruit salad and a huge slice of shoofly pie onto his plate. Silas barely tasted the food as he ate it. He tried to remember to nod and smile politely, but his thoughts were on Mary and his children as he chatted with the menfolk.

After everyone had taken their turn eating, the women brought in coffee and tea for the adults and hot chocolate for the *kinner*, and the crowd mingled beside the fireplace, among the scents of woodsmoke and strong, black coffee. The soft murmur of contented voices filled the air, but one stood out from the others. Silas's stomach dropped.

"I didn't want to *kumme* here," Becky said, loud enough for him to hear clear across the room. Mary stood beside her, clutching a mug of coffee, her face pale and drawn.

A small, elderly woman with white hair hobbled up to them, pushing people aside with her cane. The crowd moved out of her way with indulgent smiles, as if her actions were no surprise. The woman adjusted her eyeglasses and leaned forward when she reached Becky. "My name is Viola Esch. You must be Becky Hochstetler."

"Ya." Becky looked at her with surprise and a hint of shame.

"What did you just say? You don't want to be here?"

Becky swallowed hard. "*Nee.* I want to be back home in Holmes County, where I grew up."

Mary moved her hand to Becky's shoulder, but Becky shrugged it away. Silas flinched as Mary stepped back with a pained, confused expression.

"We can't always have what we want, ain't so?" Viola pointed her cane at Becky.

"*Nee*, but—"

"If *Gott* wants you here, then it's what's best for you."

"We're here because my *daed* made us move here."

"And you don't think your *daed* prayed on it?" Viola looked up and scanned the room until her eyes landed on Silas's. He nodded and she returned the nod. Silas didn't know who Viola was, but he couldn't help liking her, despite her meddling.

"*Nee*, he prayed on it, certain sure," Becky said.

"Then what's the problem?"

Becky opened her mouth, then snapped it shut again. She crossed her arms. "I just don't… I don't like it here. Everyone's been nice but…"

"Give it time," Viola said.

"I'll give it a month."

Viola squinted at Becky. "What do you mean by that?"

"If I don't like it here by the end of the month, then I'm going back to Holmes County."

"Humph." Viola gave Becky a withering look. "By yourself? How old are you? Fifteen? Sixteen?"

Becky raised her chin. "Sixteen."

Viola raised her eyes toward the ceiling. "*Youngies* today."

"I've got cousins I can live with back home," Becky said. "I should have stayed there with them." Her mouth trembled as she fought to keep her composure.

"Nee." Viola hit the hardwood floor with the bottom of her cane to emphasize her words. "You should have *kumme* here with your *daed*. What's gotten into you?"

"You don't even know me." Becky looked down as tears began to form in her eyes. She wiped them away quickly.

"Ha! I know enough, that's for certain sure." Viola stared at Becky for a moment, then shook her head. Silas wanted to sink into the floor and disappear. His failure as a father was on display for all to see. *Englisch* teenagers might push the limits, but Amish *youngies* knew better. Becky's disrespect was shocking. And what if she meant what she said? Would she really run back to Holmes County at month's end, with or without his permission?

He pushed his way through the crowd, face burning and pulse pounding. Ethan shadowed him in silence. Mary watched them coming with a worried look on her face, hands clasped tightly in front of her. He had been married less than a day and he was already failing both his daughter and his new wife.

"Becky's had a long day," Mary announced to Viola and whoever else might be listening in. "She's a *gut* girl, but she's not herself right now. She's got a lot to adjust to."

Silas felt a surge of hope at Mary's defense of his daughter. But his heart plummeted at Becky's response. "You don't know me, either," Becky snapped.

"Nee," Mary said gently. "But I'd like to."

Becky kept her eyes on the floor, arms still crossed.

Silas stepped in front of his daughter.

"I, uh… I want to thank everyone for the warm welcome. But it's time for us to get on home. It's been a long day and we traveled a long way yesterday. Becky's tired." Silas didn't know how many people were listening, but the noise level in the room had definitely dropped at Becky's outburst. He suspected the entire crowd was following the incident closely. This was no way to make a good impression on the new church district. "Do you mind if we head home?" Silas asked Mary in a low voice.

"Nee." She gave him an unexpectedly cheerful smile. "Let's get you all settled in. I'm sure everything will be just fine." Silas wondered if she meant what she said. Her smile certainly was encouraging, but he could sense the anxiety behind it. He knew he should tell her that she shouldn't feel obligated to solve his problems, but he couldn't get the words out. Instead, he led his new blended family out of the Millers's

farmhouse and into the icy air in silence, his jaw clenched and his expression hard.

Mary was sure that Silas regretted marrying her. He helped her into the buggy and asked if she was warm enough, but that was all he said. For most of the ride home, he sat hunched against the wind without speaking, his face turned to the road. Mary almost spoke to him several times as they wound past weather-beaten farmhouses with Saturday's laundry freeze-drying on the line. But no words came out. Instead, she sat as rigid as the frosty earth, unable to communicate her fears. What if she confronted Silas and he just sighed, shook his head and confirmed that he was sorry he had gone through with the wedding? It would be too much to bear. So she waited in silence, her hands clasped tightly together, the cold wind stinging her eyes. Becky was silent as well. She clutched her black cloak around her narrow shoulders and stared into the distance. Only Ethan acknowledged Mary as he sat wedged between her and Silas, when he scooted close and slipped his small arm in hers.

When they finally reached her house, Mary's new family filed out of the buggy without ceremony. Her heart sank at the lack of celebration. But then Silas walked around to her door and offered to help her to the ground. She liked how strong his bicep felt as she rested her hand on his arm and hopped down. She dropped her hand and stepped back from him. Silas hesitated. "Mary, I'm sorry I asked to leave the Millers early. You should have gotten to stay longer and enjoy your wedding day." He frowned and looked down at his feet. "It wasn't fair to you."

Was that the cause of Silas's silence? Was he feeling guilty? He turned and walked away before she could ask. Mary stood in the ankle-deep snow of her yard and pulled her cloak tighter as she watched him lead Red Rover into the barn. The buggy horse snorted and shook his head against the stranger. Silas murmured to him gently, too low for Mary to make out the words, and gave him a comforting pat on the neck. His gentleness gave Mary hope. Even if he didn't like her, he seemed to be a good man.

A small woolen mitten touched her hand and Mary looked down to see Ethan looking up at her. She was surprised that a boy his age would hover beside her, rather than follow his father into the barn, and her chest ached at how much the boy needed a mother. "Let's get you some hot chocolate, *ya*?"

Ethan nodded and almost managed a smile.

"*Kumme*, it's freezing out here," Mary said as she put an arm around him and began walking toward the front porch. She glanced behind her to watch Silas disappear inside the barn. He did not look back at her at all.

Becky wandered inside after them and Mary flashed a welcoming smile. "Join us for some hot chocolate? I've got marshmallows."

Becky just shook her head as they hung up their outerwear, then headed upstairs to her new room, each footstep falling heavily on the wooden floorboards.

"Vell," Mary said as she turned her smile toward Ethan. "We're going to have some wonderful good hot chocolate and just this once, because it's a special day, you can have as many marshmallows as you want."

Ethan hovered beside her and watched as she warmed fresh milk from Stoltzfus's dairy on the gas-powered stove, then added the cocoa powder, sugar and vanilla extract. She tore open the bag of marshmallows and handed it to Ethan as he waited. He pulled one out and nibbled it with a solemn expression on his face. "I like your kitchen," he said.

Mary beamed. "What do you like about it?"

"It has marshmallows."

Mary laughed. “What else do you like to eat? We’ll go buy groceries tomorrow.”

“I like pumpkin pie and turkey with stuffing. Most people only eat that at Thanksgiving, but I like it all year round.”

“Well, then I’ll have to cook it for you.”

Ethan’s face lit up. “For certain sure?”

“For certain sure.” Mary pulled the spoon from the pot, set it in the spoon rest and flicked off the burner. “In fact, I think I might have the ingredients to make some of that tonight for supper.”

“Can I help?”

Mary hesitated. Amish boys didn’t usually help in the kitchen once they were old enough to spend their chore time helping their fathers. She hoped Silas wouldn’t mind. “I’d like that very much,” she said.

Ethan nodded. “*Gut*. That way I can make it for myself when you’re not here anymore.”

“Ethan, I’m not going anywhere. I’m here to be your mother from now on. Didn’t your *daed* explain that to you?”

Ethan's brow creased. "*Ya*. But mothers don't stay. They always leave."

Mary's heart sank. Silas had only vaguely mentioned in his letter that Ethan's mother had passed away while he was just a baby. She didn't really know what had happened, although it was obvious that the loss still weighed heavily on the family.

Mary hoped that a big, home-cooked meal would make Ethan and the rest of the family feel welcomed. And maybe, just maybe, Silas would appreciate her efforts. Perhaps, if she worked hard enough, she could convince him to like her, just a little. Mary didn't expect a romantic relationship, but she longed to at least form a friendship with the man she had just tied herself to for life.

"I don't have a turkey," Mary said as she rummaged through the gas-powered refrigerator. "But I do have a chicken. We could roast it." She pulled out some celery and smiled. "Looks like we can throw together some stuffing, too. How about chicken with stuffing and gravy?"

Ethan rocked up onto his toes with an excited smile. "And pumpkin pie?"

"*Ya*. I've got a can of pumpkin in the larder. *Kumme*, you can help me get started on the piecrust."

Mary spent the afternoon showing Ethan how to mix dough, roll out a piecrust and chop the ingredients for stuffing. He helped by taking the crusts off the slices of stale bread and cutting the slices into little squares. Every time Mary told him he was doing a good job, he stood a little taller and smiled a little wider. When the meal was almost ready, she heard the front door open and close, followed by the stomping of boots on the hardwood floor to shake off the snow. The savory smell of roasting chicken and simmering gravy filled the little house, drawing Silas into the kitchen. "Sure smells *gut* in here," he said as he appeared in the doorway, rubbing his hands together to warm them from the cold.

"Supper is almost ready," Mary said as she closed the door to the oven, then adjusted the temperature. She turned around to see Silas staring at Ethan with a strange look on his face.

"I've been helping, *Daed*," Ethan said. A smudge of white flour covered his nose and one of Mary's worn kitchen aprons was tied around his waist. It was too big for him and fell nearly to his ankles.

"*Ya*, I can see that."

"I hope that's *oll recht*," Mary said quietly.

Silas scratched his head as his eyes moved back and forth from his son, to Mary, then back to his son again. "It's not the way things are done," he said. "*Buwe* don't help the womenfolk in the kitchen by the time they're his age. They help the men with the farm work or in the workshops."

"But I wanted to spend time with Mary. You said she's going to be my new *mamm*."

Mary stood with her hands clasped, unsure of what to say. Had she already made a mess of things? All she wanted was to do the right thing, but somehow, she was already failing.

Silas stared for another moment, then shrugged. "*Vell*, even though it's not usual, I can't see that there's anything actually wrong with it. There's no rule against it in the *Ordnung*. What do you think your bishop would say, Mary?"

Mary looked down. Her heart pounded as she spoke. "I think he would say that it's *gut* for Ethan to feel welcome in his new home and to connect with his new *mamm*."

Silas gave a decisive nod. "*Gut*. I agree."

Mary felt a wave of relief ripple through her. Most Amish men would have insisted that their sons stick to tradition, instead of understanding a wounded child's need for comfort and closeness with his new mother. She felt her heart soften toward Silas and knew she was beginning to like this stranger who seemed so full of love for his children, despite his hard demeanor. Or perhaps, that was the root of his somber, distant attitude. Pain and loss could build heavy walls around a man, even between him and the people he wanted to reach most.

"Your *sohn* has been a big help today," Mary said. "I think you'll be happy with supper."

"It's a feast, *Daed*," Ethan announced. "Just like Thanksgiving. We didn't have a turkey, but there's roast chicken instead, with stuffing and cranberry sauce and two different pies for dessert. Pumpkin and sweet-potato."

Silas's eyes moved across the stove, surveying the simmering pots, then along the counter, to the loaf of bread, fruit salad and pitcher of fresh-squeezed lemonade. Mary expected him to smile, but he frowned instead. "You've done too much, Mary. It isn't Thanksgiving."

Mary's relief was replaced by confusion. "*Nee*, but it's our wedding day." She said the words so quietly she wasn't sure Silas had heard. But then his frown deepened and she knew he had. Was he that disappointed by the marriage?

"*Ya*, but..." Silas shook his head. "Never mind."

"You don't like Thanksgiving food? Ethan said it's his favorite. But if you don't like it, I've got some church spread in the larder to go with the bread and I can make you some soup."

Silas's frown shifted to remorse. "*Nee*. I don't want you to make me soup. This meal is fine. It's *gut*. Too *gut*. What I meant is that you shouldn't have gone to all the trouble. I didn't expect for you to do all this for me. I'm not here to..." Silas's eyes cut to his son. "I mean... *Danki*."

Mary couldn't understand what she had done wrong. Didn't Silas want his wife to cook a big meal for him? She wanted to show him that she was worth marrying and this was the best way that she knew how. But now she could see that it was not enough. The old, familiar doubt in her own abilities crept up her spine. "I'm sorry, Silas. I don't know—"

"Why are you apologizing, Mary? There's no reason for that."

Mary couldn't read his expression. It could have been disappointment, or something else she didn't have a word for. Something closer to empathy.

"You've done too much," Silas added.

You've done too much. The sentence rang in Mary's head as she tried to interpret it. She was perplexed. Her father and brother had always assumed that they were entitled to big, homecooked meals every day.

"Can we eat now?" Ethan asked. "I'm starving and it looks so *gut*."

"Ya," Mary said quickly, relieved by the distraction. "Go fetch your *schwester*."

Ethan barreled out of the room, leaving Mary alone with Silas. She turned to the stove and began scooping up creamed corn into a serving dish to keep from having to face her new husband.

She heard Silas take a step closer to her. "Mary, I…"

Mary hesitated, then turned around, the serving spoon still in her hand. Silas looked surprisingly vulnerable. Her eyes met his and she felt the emotion behind them for a moment, before a wall slammed down and his expression hardened. "Never mind. Let's eat, *ya*?"

"*Ya*. I hope you like it."

"I'm sure I will." But his voice sounded sad, rather than pleased. Mary couldn't bear feeling as though she wasn't living up to his expectations. The feeling was like an itch under her skin, tormenting her to do something. "I guess I'm not what you expected, but maybe things are better than you realize," she blurted out before she could stop herself. "I know we've only just met. But Ethan is such a sweet *bu* and I already feel like I'm reaching him. I want to be the *mamm* he needs. This marriage, it's about more than just that, though, ain't so?" She shifted her weight from one foot to the other and looked away. "I haven't been courted since I was twenty years old. I saw the letter in *The Budget* and I knew…well…" Mary dropped her gaze and tried to hide the hope in her voice. "That it felt right, *ya*?"

Silas looked into her eyes with an unreadable expression. Mary's mouth went dry. She had said too much.

"Mary, I really appreciate the big meal and everything you've done for me. But I'm afraid you've got the wrong idea." Silas's voice faltered. "It's my fault. I should have been clearer."

Mary's brow creased as she stared up at him. She had not been this close to him before. He smelled of leather and soap, and had a faint sprinkle of freckles across his tanned nose, along with chiseled cheekbones. She had a silly impulse to step closer, but forced it away. "What do you mean?"

Silas closed his eyes and pinched the bridge of his nose, then dropped his hand and opened his eyes to stare down at her. "This is a business arrangement, Mary. It can only ever be a business arrangement between us." He looked like he wanted to say more, but he shook his head instead. "I'm so sorry, Mary. That's all I can give you."

Mary stared up at him without speaking. There were no words for the humiliation and disappointment searing through her. Her brother and father had been right all along.

She wasn't good enough.

And now, she was married to someone who thought that. Forever.

Chapter Four

Mary spent the next morning cooking and cleaning while Becky avoided her and Silas stayed in the barn. She knew he needed to convert the space into a harness shop right away, but his absence still stung. She didn't know what she had expected, but it certainly wasn't to feel as alone after her marriage as she had before it. Perhaps Amos's warning had been accurate. The thought had chilled her all day, despite the warmth from the woodstove that heated the rooms of her little house.

That afternoon, the happy sound of clip-clopping horse hooves and a child's laughter drifted inside. Mary's heart leaped at the thought of visitors and she couldn't race to the door fast enough. She flung it open to see her nephew, Gabriel, his new wife, Eliza, and their six-year-old foster daughter, Priss, tumbling out of their buggy, each of them bundled against the cold.

Mary waved and Gabriel grinned at her before leading his horse into the barn, where he would put her in a warm stall with a serving of oats while the family visited. Mary tensed as she wondered how he and Silas would get along. Gabriel was outgoing and fun-loving, the opposite of her new husband, from what little she could make out about him so far.

Eliza and Priss hurried across the yard, racing against the sharp, icy wind to the front porch. Mary motioned them inside and they swept into the living room along with a gust of cold air. "*Kumme* in and have some hot *kaffi*," Mary said as she gave them each a big hug.

"Can I say hello to Becky and Ethan?" Priss asked as she looked up at Mary with big brown eyes. Her chubby cheeks were so adorable that Mary had to give her another hug before she sent her upstairs to find Becky.

"She's folding laundry so I'm sure she'd appreciate some help. Ethan's helping his *daed* in the barn, but I'm sure they'll *kumme* back to the house to see you all. It's time for an afternoon *kaffi* break, anyway."

"Ya," Eliza said as she hung her black winter cloak on a peg by the door. "We just finished our work for the day at the Millers's and thought it would be a *gut* time to *kumme*." Eliza worked in Aunt Fannie's Amish Gift Shop and Gabriel worked on the Miller farm, where they had fallen in love despite being complete opposites. Their love story had given Mary hope that perhaps true love really could overcome all obstacles.

"It's *gut* to see you both," Mary said to

Eliza as Priss trotted up the stairs. "The house is so quiet today."

Eliza frowned. "You're feeling lonely even though you have a new family?"

"Oh." Mary flinched. Eliza was notoriously forward, but this was too much even for her.

Eliza pushed her big round glasses up the bridge of her nose as she stared at Mary. "I said too much, didn't I? If Gabriel were here, he would tell me to be more thoughtful about what I say." She flashed an impish grin. "But then I would say back to him, what's wrong with getting the truth out on the table? Best just get on with it, *ya*?"

Mary smiled. "You and Gabriel are *gut* together. You balance each other."

"You're avoiding my question."

"*Ya*. I am." Mary headed toward the kitchen. "Let's get that *kaffi*."

Eliza raised an eyebrow and followed Mary. "Are you unhappy with the match? Has he been unkind to you?"

Mary let out a sharp sigh. She didn't want to tell Eliza how she felt, but at the same time, it was a relief to get her feelings out. "*Nee*, he seems to be a *gut* man. I think his bishop and church elders were right to vouch for him."

"Then what's the matter? And don't tell me nothing, because I can tell that you're upset."

"*Ach*, I don't know. It's complicated." Mary pulled the metal tin of coffee grounds from the cabinet as Eliza poured water into the kettle and flicked on the burner.

Eliza turned to Mary. "Does he treat you well? Do you like him? I think it's pretty straightforward."

Mary laughed. "It's absurd how simple you make it all sound!"

Eliza wiped her hands on her apron, then straightened it against her rail-thin frame. "I think it's absurd how complicated you make things. Do you like him or not?"

Mary glanced toward the empty doorway, then back at Eliza. "Of course, I do," she hissed in a low whisper. "He's exactly the kind of man I've hoped for—hard-working, *gut* to his *kinner*, devoted to family and kind to animals."

"And kind to you?"

Mary looked away. "*Ya*. But..."

Eliza's eyes narrowed from behind her big round glasses. "But what?"

"It's just that..." Mary twisted her hands together. "I don't think he likes me."

"*Ach*, Mary. You don't think anyone likes you."

Mary's mouth opened, then closed again. Did she really think that? "*Nee*. That's not true."

Eliza peered down her nose at Mary.

"I can get insecure sometimes..."

"I can understand that. I never thought Gabriel could love someone like me. He's so popular and *gut*-looking and I'm just... well, me. I've never been popular and I've never been considered pretty."

"Gabriel loves you for who you are."

"Exactly. So will Silas. You've got a lot to offer, Mary."

"I've been trying to show him that. I cooked a huge meal last night—it took hours—but he wasn't happy about it."

"That's not what I mean by having a lot to offer."

"*Vell*, I also scrubbed the house from top to bottom before he got here and redid the upstairs rooms so they would be perfect for him and his *kinner*. But he didn't seem to appreciate that, either. I don't know what more I can do to earn his love."

"Mary."

Mary jumped when he suddenly heard her name. Spinning around, she saw Gabriel standing in the doorway.

"I wish you could hear yourself."

"Silas? Is he here with you?" She craned her neck to see behind Gabriel, panicked that her new husband had overheard her.

"*Nee*, he's finishing up in the barn, but he'll be in soon."

Mary exhaled and waited for her heart to slow back down to normal.

"So what's this about earning love?" Gabriel said as he casually strode across the kitchen and pulled out a chair from the dinette table.

"It's nothing," Mary said.

Gabriel dropped into the chair, leaned back and propped his feet up on the opposite chair. "Don't worry, I took my boots off at the door." He flashed a mischievous grin. "I know how you love to complain about shoes on the furniture."

Mary rolled her eyes but couldn't help but smile.

"You know you miss me," Gabriel said.

"I don't miss being interrogated," Mary retorted.

"Right. About that. You've got it all wrong, as usual."

"You're one to talk," Mary said.

Gabriel hesitated, then his expression shifted from playfulness to seriousness. "*Ach, vell,* maybe I can relate."

Mary sighed. "I know you can," she said softly.

"Love that has to be earned isn't love at all." Gabriel looked away. "My father has made that clear enough."

"Ya," Mary said. "And my father before him."

The atmosphere in the room suddenly grew awkward and sad, and Mary didn't know what else to say. "I don't know what I'd do without you," she finally admitted.

Gabriel flashed his signature grin. "*Vell*, for starters you wouldn't have to worry about muddy boots on your furniture."

Mary laughed. It felt good to release the tension. Gabriel always knew how to do that. "I've missed you, Gabriel."

"Of course, you have, *Aenti*. Now, how about some pie to go with that *kaffi*?" He patted his stomach. "I've worked up a powerful *gut* appetite today."

"You always have a powerful *gut* appetite," Mary said, but her eyes were smiling as she opened the pie safe and pulled out the leftover sweet-potato pie from the previous night.

Just then, the front door opened and the house filled with the sound of voices murmuring in the living room. "There should be enough pie for everyone," Mary said. "And the water's boiling so I can brew the *kaffi*." She was glad to have something to do. It would keep her from having to look at Silas or speak to him. She felt too unsure of herself to do either.

Becky and Priss trotted down the stairs a moment later. "We heard *Daed kumme* in," Becky said as she entered the kitchen. "Priss said there's *kaffi*. Can we have some pie with it?"

Mary gave her a welcoming smile. "*Ya*. We've already gotten the leftover sweet-potato pie out and I've got a tin of homemade snickerdoodles, too." Mary reached across the counter for the cookie tin when a deep, male voice boomed across the room.

"Who is this sweet girl? What a nice

smile. You must be Mary's niece." Mary could hear the kindness in Silas's voice and it warmed her all the way to her toes. It was thoughtful of him to show such care for her family, when he barely knew any of them. "It's *gut* to see you again." He nodded to Gabriel and Eliza from across the room. They had met briefly after the wedding service.

"How are you liking Bluebird Hills?" Gabriel asked as the coffee dripped slowly into the carafe. Mary wished she had more to do with her hands. She hoped no one knew how anxious she was at the thought that Silas might not be happy here, with her. She felt responsible, somehow, even though she had no control over the rest of the community, or whether or not Silas felt at home with their friends and neighbors.

"I'll serve the pie," Mary murmured, and began pulling plates from the cabinet.

"It's a nice place," Silas said. "Everyone's been welcoming. And you should have seen the feast Mary cooked last night for us."

Mary felt un unexpected rush of joy. She had not expected Silas to compliment her.

Gabriel nodded. "That sounds like Mary."

Priss and Ethan came over to the counter for the first slices of pie while Becky hung back in the doorway, watching the adults while chewing on a thumbnail. The two children devoured their slices almost immediately, then approached Mary as she poured the coffee into several mugs. "Can we go outside and play in the snow?" Ethan asked. "I finished all my chores today."

"If it's *oll recht* with your *daed* and with Priss's parents," Mary said.

"As long as you wear your mittens and stay away from the road," Eliza said to Priss.

Silas hesitated.

"Please, *Daed*?"

"Ya, oll recht." But his expression looked concerned at the thought.

The children didn't wait for him to change his mind and ran out of the room. They hurriedly jumped into their winter coats, hats and gloves, then after a few moments, the door slammed shut. The kitchen stayed snug and warm as Mary passed around mugs of coffee. She turned to tidy the counters when Silas patted the chair beside him. "*Kumme* sit, Mary."

"*Ach*, *vell*, I was going to wash the carafe."

"Silas is right, Mary," Gabriel said. "Sit and visit for a minute. We won't stay long."

"Oh, but why don't you stay for supper? Then we can really catch up."

"We can't tonight. So *kumme* sit with us while we're here."

"Oll recht." But as soon as Mary sat down, she became too aware of Silas's presence beside her. She noticed he smelled like leather and woodsmoke, and when he reached for his mug, his hand brushed her sleeve. She felt a jolt of warmth zip up her arm. She felt hyperaware of everything

he did, as though she was a schoolgirl obsessing over her first crush. Ridiculous. Especially after Silas had made it clear that this was only a business arrangement between them. She kept her eyes on her own mug and tried to pretend that she was not thinking about Silas. She wasn't even sure how she felt about him, after all. She barely knew him.

Becky ate her pie standing up at the counter, then disappeared upstairs with her coffee. Gabriel tried to chat with Silas about an upcoming horse auction, but Silas kept shifting restlessly in his chair. After a few minutes he stood up, carried his half-empty mug to the kitchen and dumped the contents down the sink. "I'm going to check on the *kinner*. It's been *gut* to visit. *Danki* for stopping by." Then he stepped out of the room.

Mary felt stung by his abrupt departure. "I'm sorry," she said as soon as she heard him leave the house. "I'm sure he didn't mean to be rude."

"You shouldn't apologize for other people," Gabriel said. "You can't control what he does."

Mary pressed her lips together and looked down. It felt like his actions were her responsibility, whether or not that made sense. She forced her chin back up. "You're right. It's just hard to see that, sometimes."

Gabriel gave a thoughtful nod. "You know that my *daed* always made me feel the same way—like everything was my fault. But it's not. And if you keep believing that way, it can push people away who care about you."

Mary wondered if she was misinterpreting Silas because of her own past. She wanted to tell Gabriel and Eliza what he had said about their marriage being a business arrangement only, and ask their opinion about that, but she was too embarrassed.

Gabriel stood up and walked out of the room.

"Now, where's he going?" Eliza wondered aloud. "No one wants to sit and have *kaffi* today?"

She and Mary followed Gabriel and found him peering out of the living-room window, into the front yard. "He seems like a *gut daed*, Mary. Not like mine or yours. Look." He scooted over to make space for Mary. She crowded beside him, while Eliza stood on her tiptoes to see over Mary's shoulder. They watched Silas making a snowman with Priss and Ethan. After a moment, Ethan grinned and threw a snowball at his father. Silas retaliated by picking up his son and swinging him around, then dropping him in a snowbank as they both howled with laughter. Mary's heart swelled at the tender scene. She had dreamed for years that she would have a husband who treated their children just like this. The thought made her turn away from the window. She couldn't watch while feeling like an outsider within her own family.

"Maybe he was just worried about his

sohn, and that's why he didn't visit with us," Eliza said. "It's a big adjustment for Ethan, losing his home, moving to a new church district and getting a new mother all in the same week."

"Ya," Mary said. "That must be it. I shouldn't assume he's trying to avoid me." But everything inside of her screamed that he was. No matter what Eliza and Gabriel said—and no matter how much she wanted to believe them—she knew the problem was her. Silas had stayed in the barn all day, then barely stayed inside for coffee. The obvious reason was that he wanted to put distance between them. After all, spending time together wasn't required in a business arrangement. Was it?

Silas didn't know what to do. Mary wouldn't stop running around, waiting on him hand and foot. He wished she could let herself relax. She jumped up every time he came in the room, offering to fetch him something to eat or pour him a cup of coffee. It bothered him to see her so uncomfortable in her own home. He wanted a partner—even if just a business partner—not a maid. He had managed to get her to sit down when Gabriel and Eliza came to visit the day before, but that had created its own problems. She had sat close enough for him to smell her lavender-scented soap and see the little lines at the corner of her eyes. Those lines meant that she laughed a lot and he liked that about her. But it also reminded him that she had barely smiled around him. It was clear that she regretted marrying him.

And why shouldn't she? He frowned too much. He stumbled over his words, until hard silences separated them. But it wasn't because he was unhappy with Mary. He wasn't frowning at her. He was frowning because he was worried about her. He wanted her to stop trying so hard to prove herself to him. He just didn't know how to tell her that.

Yesterday, as they had sat side by side,

sipping coffee, all he had been able to think about was how much he wanted to make her smile and breathe in that lovely lavender scent. But that was impossible. There was a good reason why he needed to keep his distance from her and he couldn't weaken his resolve, for her sake as much as his.

If only he could make his thoughts about Mary disappear today. Even now, as he worked to clear the barn to make space for his harness shop, she was on his mind. Her soft voice, intelligent eyes and gentle nature were all he could think about. When he agreed to this marriage, he had not considered that he might actually develop feelings for his bride. That was not part of his plan. The whole point of an arranged marriage had been to eliminate the possibility of feelings for one another.

And yet, here he was, stacking lumber in the corner of the barn while thinking about the wife he was not supposed to be thinking about.

"Silas?" The door to the barn creaked open and Mary crept inside, clutching her black cloak tightly against her chest.

Silas felt a flicker of joy at seeing her and immediately pushed the emotion down. "*Ya?* Do you need help with something?"

"Me? *Ach, nee*. I came to see if I could help you."

"Oh." Silas cleared his throat and turned his attention back to the lumber in his arms. "Nothing you can do. I'm just hauling the last of this wood you've got stored in here."

Mary surveyed the space around her. "Looks like it's time to start organizing how to set up the shop. I could help with that. I'm not bad at figuring out how to fit a lot of stuff in a small space. This barn isn't very big." She studied the freshly swept floor and the stack of lumber, feed sacks and bales of hay that were neatly lined up against the far wall. "You've been working really hard. It looks like a different place already."

Silas couldn't help but smile. "*Danki*. I think this place will do nicely for my harness shop."

"I was afraid it wouldn't be *gut* enough for you."

Silas wished that Mary felt more secure around him. He remembered how her brother had talked about her and suspected that she was still living under the weight of her family's criticism. Silas wanted to tell her that she didn't have to bear that weight anymore. But how could he put that into words?

"Why would you think that, Mary? It's a nice, snug little barn. You can barely feel the cold with the propane heater going. And with just one horse in here, it isn't crowded at all."

Mary flashed a relieved smile. "That's very *gut* to hear."

Silas set down the last load of lumber, straightened his back and stretched. "I've got all my equipment over there, ready to set up." He nodded toward a handful of crates stacked in the middle of the floor. He had shipped them before he left Sugarcreek and they had just arrived.

"It's a mercy that you could save it all."

"*Ya.* We lost everything else, but the firefighters managed to put out the fire before it burned the equipment and supplies. Some of it has a little water damage, but I think I can salvage most of it."

She nodded toward the empty wall opposite the door. "We could use that lumber to make shelves and tables there, on the far side of the barn from Red Rover's stall." The horse whinnied at the sound of his name and shook his mane. Mary laughed. "He agrees with me."

Silas smiled. "Because it's a *gut* idea."

Mary blushed and Silas could see that his compliment made her uncomfortable. He wanted to say more to her, but didn't want to make her feel even more awkward. "*Danki* for your help."

"I'll get the bucket and mop and scrub down this floor while you get started on building the tables." She hesitated. "Then maybe I can help with that, too…"

"I'd like that." He meant the words, even though he had not intended to say them out loud. The last thing he wanted was to draw closer to Mary by working side by side. And yet, he couldn't resist her sweet offer. The thought of spending the afternoon together hammering, sawing and chatting made him smile inside. He liked Mary. She was far more thoughtful than he had expected her to be. And he would rather she work in the barn, with him, than tire herself out doing unnecessary jobs elsewhere. He appreciated all the baking and cooking she was doing for him, but there was only so much room in his stomach and he didn't want to offend her by refusing one of her made-from-scratch pies. This way they could relax and get to know each other— He cut off the thought and frowned.

This was not going the way he had

planned. Maintaining his distance was getting harder.

And maintaining that distance got even more difficult as they spent the next few hours together. Mary was so enjoyable to be around, once she let down her guard and began to talk to him. "Where would you go, if you could go anywhere?" he asked as she sanded a board that he had just measured and cut.

She cocked her head to the side as she considered the question. The sound of sandpaper rasping against wood filled the barn, alongside Red Rover's chomping as he ate his oats. "*Ach*, I don't know," Mary said after a moment. "I've never thought about going anywhere. I've dreamed about what might happen here, in my own little house, rather than where I might go."

Silas marked a place on a two-by-four with a pencil, then released the measuring tape in his hand. He set the tape on the two-by-four and glanced over at her. A thin beam of sunshine shone through the barn window, highlighting dust motes in the air and bathing her face in a yellow glow. She looked so beautiful in that moment—so fragile and full of dreams—that it made his chest ache. He looked away quickly and picked up the handsaw. "What have you dreamed might happen here?" he asked, even though he feared that her answer would tug dangerously at his heart.

Mary smiled sadly to herself before she answered. "It's silly. I just always dreamed that..." She swallowed hard. "That my home would be full of people who loved me." She set down the sandpaper and straightened up so fast that she lost her balance and stumbled. Silas reached out and grabbed her elbow to steady her. Her dark gray eyes shot to his and, for an instant, Silas sensed all of the longing locked away inside. He wanted to pull her closer, and whisper that he and his children would love her, that her dream was not silly, that she was worth loving. But instead, he steadied her until he was sure she had regained her footing, then released her and stepped back.

Her cheeks flushed red. "I, uh… I should see to supper. It's getting late, *ya*?"

He stared at her, trying to form the right words while keeping the emotional distance he knew he must. Before he could get anything out, the barn door creaked open and Becky appeared in the entrance, her thin silhouette backlit by the weak January sun.

"What are you doing?" his daughter asked as she stepped forward, frowning.

"Making progress on my workshop," Silas said. "Looks *gut*, ain't so?"

The frown did not leave Becky's face as her eyes swept across the barn. "You should have let me help, *Daed*."

"You were busy helping Mary in the kitchen."

"*Ya*, until Mary left me alone to do it."

"Oh." Mary's cheeks became even redder.

A flicker of pain shot through Silas at

Mary's expression. She looked so vulnerable and embarrassed.

"I'm sorry," Mary said quickly. "I just came to check on how your *daed* was doing and then, before I knew it…"

Silas knew that after Amish girls finished the eighth grade and left school, they were expected to work full time at domestic chores, or to hire themselves out as housekeepers until they married. But he had noticed that Mary went easy on Becky, cutting her plenty of slack while she adjusted, even though most Amish families would expect a daughter to be as capable as an adult by her age.

"I'm not sure you're being fair, Becky," Silas said gently. "You did all the cooking at home. I know you can handle it. In fact, you always said you liked being in charge of the kitchen."

"Ya," Becky admitted with a reluctant tone. She seemed to recognize that she had lost that battle, but Silas could tell she was gearing up for the next volley. Becky

stepped closer and squinted at the board that Mary had been sanding. “You haven’t even done that much.”

“Becky,” Silas said with quiet authority.

But Becky did not stop. “I bet you don’t even know how to use a hammer properly. I could have done a lot more than you in here, and I could have done it a lot quicker, too. I’ve been helping *Daed* for years in his shop.”

“That’s enough, Becky,” Silas said.

“It’s *oll recht*, Silas,” Mary said. “She’s just telling the truth. I’m no carpenter. I shouldn’t have tried to help.” She stepped back. “Here, Becky. You can take over my job.”

“*Nee*, Mary.” Silas shook his head. “That isn’t true.” He turned to Becky. “You can’t talk to her that way, *dochder*.”

Becky stared at him. Behind the fire in her eyes he could see the hidden pain. Her lips trembled almost imperceptibly, but Silas noticed. Ever since she was a toddler, Becky had done that when she was about to cry. A great weariness flooded him, until his chest felt too heavy to carry his emotions. What could he say to get through to his daughter and make sure she treated Mary kindly? How could he be there for both of them when Becky wanted to push everyone away and when he was too afraid to tell Mary how he really felt?

"She doesn't know what she's doing, *Daed*."

"Go back to the house, Becky," Silas said firmly. "Stay in your room until you hear from me."

Becky crossed her arms and stared at him.

"Now."

Becky heaved a dramatic sigh, turned on her heel and stormed out of the barn.

Mary hesitated, then began walking to the door after Becky. She stopped and turned back to Silas. "She's just feeling left out, that's all. She doesn't want to be replaced."

"It's no excuse for talking that way to you."

"You're right. It's not. But…"

Silas stared at Mary. He felt a deep sadness that even now, after being berated by a sixteen-year-old, she wouldn't stand up for herself. His brief meeting with Elmo had been all he needed to understand why. "But what?" he asked when she didn't finish her sentence. He realized that he was frowning and tried to soften his expression. He was angry—angry at the situation, at his daughter for her outburst, at his late wife for abandoning him and his children, at Mary's family for hurting her—but not at Mary. He could not imagine being angry with her.

She looked down and studied her hands. "Nothing. I shouldn't have said anything. I shouldn't interfere. I hope I didn't make a mess of things in here. I'll go finish getting supper on, like I should have earlier."

"Mary, please stop this."

Her eyes flicked up to his with a look of surprise.

"Can't you…?" He struggled for the right words, then blurted them out before he could stop himself. "Can't you see that you're good enough?" He swallowed hard. "More than good enough. You're…really special." Silas felt unmasked, exposed. Had he said too much? He was supposed to keep his feelings reined in, not admit to Mary how he really felt about her.

Mary's mouth opened as if to speak, but nothing came out. She just stared at him as she closed her mouth. A small, sad smile turned up the corner of her lips. *"Nee,"* she murmured. "I can't." Then she turned and walked out before he could stop her.

Silas kept his eyes on the empty doorway for a long time, unable to forget Mary's expression or her words. He had to help her and his daughter somehow.

But he had no idea how.

Chapter Five

Mary hovered outside Becky's room for a moment before knocking on the door. Her instincts told her this was a bad idea, but she had to do something. She hadn't been able to sleep all night. Instead, she had replayed their conversation in her mind as she listened to a branch scratch against her window. She had felt completely alone in her dark, first floor bedroom, even though three other people slept peacefully in the rooms above her. This was not what having a family of her own was supposed to feel like.

So she had decided to do the only thing

she could—reach out to Becky to make her feel loved and wanted, no matter what it took. Taking a deep breath, Mary squared her shoulders and knocked.

"Who's there?" Becky called out.

"It's me—Mary."

Becky sighed loudly enough for Mary to hear it through the door. "What do you want?"

Mary cringed. She had never heard an Amish child talk to an elder this way. It was unheard of, really. But Mary couldn't bring herself to blame Becky for it. The child was hurting, obviously. And Mary couldn't help but feel that maybe, it was somehow her own fault. If she just tried harder to connect with her, then surely everything would be okay. "Can I *kumme* in?"

There was another sharp sigh. *"Ya."*

Mary eased open the door and smiled. Becky did not smile back. She didn't even look up, but kept her attention on the stocking she was darning. Mary didn't let

Becky's reaction stop her. She crossed the room and sat down on Ethan's bed. The metal springs creaked beneath her weight. "Ethan's been in the barn all morning helping your *daed*. He'll have to start school soon, but we're giving him a few days to adjust." Mary paused to let the words sink in. "It's hard adjusting to a new place, ain't so?"

"I guess so," Becky murmured, her attention still on the black stocking in her hand.

"Especially when there're new people to get used to."

Becky made a sound of frustration in her throat. "Are you talking about yourself? I'm not a child, you know. You can just say what you're thinking."

"I think it isn't easy for you to have a stepmother."

Becky shrugged as she pulled her needle through the toe of the stocking.

"It would have been hard for me, for certain sure," Mary said. "Especially at your age."

"I told you, I'm *not* a child."

"*Nee*. Which makes it even harder."

Becky's eyes shot up in surprise.

Mary smiled. "I remember what it feels like to be sixteen, even if you can't imagine that."

"You don't know what any of this is like for me."

"*Nee*, I suppose not. Everyone's experience is different. But I do know what it feels like to be alone, even when you're surrounded by other people." Mary ran her finger along the edges of a blue star on the quilt covering the bed as she debated whether to say more. "That's the loneliest feeling of all." Becky didn't say anything, which Mary took as a good sign. She could tell the girl was listening to her.

"Now," Mary said and stood up abruptly. "It's time for an outing. You'd like that, *ya*?"

Becky dropped the stocking onto the bed beside her. For the first time, Mary appeared to have her full attention. "Where would we go?"

"Is that the only pair of stockings you have?"

"*Ya*. And they have a hole in them."

"Everything else was lost in the fire?"

"*Ya*. Everything but the clothes we were wearing. Some people in our old church district donated a few things to help us get by temporarily, but none of them fit very well."

"Right. Time to go to the fabric store so we can make you a new wardrobe."

Becky gave Mary the first genuine smile she had seen from her. "Really?"

"Sure."

"Right now?"

"Right now."

Twenty minutes later, Mary was guiding Red Rover into the parking lot of Beiler's Quilt and Fabric Shop. The storefront, with its row of discount fabrics on display in the windows, felt as familiar as her own home. A wave of longing washed over Mary. She knew Betty Beiler had not wanted to let her go—at least she knew it intellectually. But her body said otherwise. She could still feel the rejection deep down, in the pit of her stomach.

"I thought you wanted to bring me here," Becky said from the passenger side of the bench seat. She crossed her arms and looked away, toward an *Englisch* family in bright winter coats hurrying into the coffee shop next door.

"I do," Mary said as she pulled on the reins. The horse shook his head and stomped a hoof before allowing the buggy to stop. "But Red Rover doesn't."

"Is that supposed to be a joke?" Becky asked without turning back toward Mary. Her eyes were following the movement of shoppers bustling along the sidewalk. They wore fur-lined boots and winter hats, and held to-go cups with the name of the coffee shop printed on them.

Mary sighed. This outing was already feeling like a bad idea and they weren't even inside the store yet. "*Ya*, I guess it was a joke. And I do want to bring you here. It's just that I worked here for a long time and now I don't anymore. I haven't been back since..."

"Since you quit?" Becky's head swiveled to Mary. "Or since you got fired?" Her eyes narrowed. "You got fired, didn't you?"

"*Ach, nee*. Not exactly." Mary felt a familiar rush of shame color her cheeks.

"Not exactly? Did you or didn't you?"

Mary didn't answer.

Becky's eyes sparkled. "What did you do? I thought you were so *gut* and perfect, but maybe you've got a bad side, *ya*?"

Mary couldn't help but laugh at such a ludicrous thought. "You think I'm perfect?"

Becky frowned. "That's not what I meant. *Vell*, not exactly. I mean, you do everything just right, ain't so? You're always cooking and cleaning and trying to make *Daed* happy."

"You noticed that?"

"*Ya*. Who wouldn't?"

"And you're criticizing me for it? Don't

you want *gut* home-cooked meals and a clean house? Don't you want your *daed* to be happy?"

Becky shrugged. "I don't know." She nibbled on her thumbnail. "I just don't think that's making *Daed* happy. And I don't like the way it makes me feel."

Mary frowned. "I don't understand."

"*Daed* knows how to take care of himself. We all do. *Mamm*'s been gone nearly my whole life."

"Oh. *Oll recht*." Mary studied Becky's expression closely, trying to decipher her thoughts. "What did you mean when you said you don't like the way I make you feel?"

"I don't like feeling like I have to do a bunch of stuff to get *Daed*'s attention. I just want him to notice me for being me."

Mary flinched. Was that really how she was making Becky feel? "I didn't..."

"I can't be like you," Becky said as a mask of defiance slammed across her face.

"*Nee*, you shouldn't try to be. I mean

why… Why would you want to?" Mary felt confused and frustrated. No matter how hard she tried she couldn't seem to please anyone.

"Because *Daed* likes you."

Mary shook her head. Where could she even begin? She wanted to explain that Silas did not like her, but it wouldn't be right to put the burden of that knowledge on the girl. "Becky, how your *daed* feels about me has nothing to do with how he feels about you."

Becky glared at Mary. "Of course, it does. He wants me to be like you."

"*Nee*, I promise you that's not true."

"Nothing I do is *gut* enough for him."

Mary's heart constricted. She knew exactly how that felt. But Silas seemed so loving, unlike Mary's father. He had been harsh and demanding, not gentle and thoughtful, like Silas. Even so, being a sixteen-year-old girl wasn't easy, especially a motherless one trying to navigate a new life in the midst of strangers. Mary put her hand on Becky's arm, but Becky shook it off. Mary ignored the slight. "I don't think that's true, Becky. What makes you believe that?"

"I don't know."

"Try to explain."

"I said I don't know. And, anyway, why should I try to explain? Why do you care?" Becky rubbed her hands together and blew on her fingers to warm them. Behind the scowl on her face, Mary could see the pain in the girl's eyes. She knew they weren't getting anywhere and she ached with frustration. "Let's get inside. It's too cold to sit in the buggy."

"Fine," Becky said. She pushed open the door, slid to the ground with a thump and trudged into the shop without looking back to see if Mary was following. Mary sighed, took a moment to fasten Red Rover to the hitching post and pat him on the neck, then followed Becky into the shop. The safe, familiar smell of fabric fresh from the factory filled her nose.

A handful of Amish women murmured in the corner as they ran their fingers over a bolt of blue cotton-polyester blend. Mary knew exactly how much it cost per yard. She knew everything about the store.

"Mary!" Betty Beiler's voice echoed across the shop as she rushed over. "It's so *gut* to see you."

Mary forced a smile. She was glad to see her old friend, but still felt awkward and unwanted, despite the warm welcome. "Hi, Betty. How is business?"

"*Ach*, you know how it is. Same as it has been." Betty pressed her hand against her forehead and shook her head. "*Nee*, that's not true. Nothing is the same without you."

Mary stood silent, not knowing how to respond to her former employer.

Betty fidgeted with the big silver sewing scissors in her hand. "I feel so bad that I had to let you go, Mary."

Mary noticed that the hair peeking out from Betty's *kapp* looked a little grayer than before. And she had lost her familiar, cheerful smile. "Betty, how are you feeling? Are you *oll recht*?"

"*Ach*, I'm fine."

Mary put a hand on Betty's arm. "*Nee*. Really, Betty. How are you?"

Betty let out a long breath and shook her head. "I could use a rest, to tell you the truth. It's been a lot of stress trying to compete with the Sew-N-Save. And I just feel so guilty about having to let you go… I haven't felt quite the same since."

Mary let the words sink in. "You feel that bad about my leaving?"

"For certain sure, I do."

Mary frowned. She let go of Betty's arm and looked down. "I…"

"Mary, you didn't think I *wanted* you to leave, did you?"

"Not exactly, it's just…"

Betty clicked her tongue. "*Ach*, Mary."

Mary didn't look up. The question made her too uncomfortable.

"Childhood lasts such a short time, but it stays with us for the rest of our lives."

Mary's eyes shot up to Betty's.

"You know, I knew your father. We weren't that far apart in age. And your brother..." Betty's mouth drew into a tight line and she hesitated before continuing. "*Vell,* it was clear how they treated you. I don't want you to feel rejected by me, too. I really appreciate you, Mary. I really do."

An awkward silence stretched between them. Mary felt embarrassed and relieved to know that Betty understood. *"Danki,"* she whispered as she cut her eyes across the store, hoping that Becky had not overheard. Fortunately, she was too busy studying the bolts of fabric.

"But now you have a husband and a family of your own, ain't so? This could be a chance for a new start, even if it was an unusual way to come together."

Mary let out a long, slow breath. "I hope so, Betty, but I just don't know..."

Betty looked concerned. She began to speak, but Becky interrupted her. "Mary?" Becky spoke loud enough for her voice to carry across the shop. "I like this one."

Mary and Betty both turned their attention to Becky. Mary wondered what Betty had been about to say, but didn't want to press the issue. It was too embarrassing. She didn't want anyone to know that her new start had not been very good so far. "We've got a lot of shopping to do," Mary said. "The whole family needs new clothes. They lost everything in the fire, you know."

"*Ya*, so I've heard."

"Word travels fast through the Amish telegraph," Mary said.

"Gossip, you mean." Betty snorted. "People are talking, of course."

"I can only imagine." Mary lowered her voice and moved her gaze from Becky back to Betty. "What are they saying?"

Betty shook her head. "Don't you worry about that. It doesn't matter."

"*Ya*, it does!"

"*Nee*. It doesn't. You just do what is right for you, Mary. And prove to them it's right by how well you live your life. Be happy with your new family. That'll show everyone that says otherwise."

It felt strange to even *imagine* not caring about what people thought. "I wish I could do that."

Betty chuckled and threw an arm around Mary's shoulder. "Easier said than done, for certain sure." She squeezed Mary to emphasize her words and her affection.

"For certain sure," Mary repeated.

"Mary?" Becky called out again from across the store.

"*Ach*, *vell*, I've got to get this shopping done." Mary paused and bit her lip. "*Danki*, Betty. I appreciate what you've said."

Betty smiled. "Let me know if you two need any help, although I'm sure you know your way around this place better than I do."

As Mary strode across the store to Becky, the ache in the pit of her stomach didn't feel so sharp anymore.

"I want this for a new dress," Becky said and pointed to a bolt of vivid turquoise fabric.

Mary glanced at the color and shook her

head. "I'm sorry, you'll have to choose another. This one is too bright for our church district's *Ordnung*. A softer blue would be *oll recht* though."

"I want this one. I could have worn it back home."

"*Ya*. The rules are a little stricter here, I guess. We don't wear that color."

"Then why do they carry it here?"

"It's popular with the *Englischers*."

Becky folded her arms and turned away.

Mary scanned the row of fabric. "How about this one?" She rubbed a length of pale blue fabric between her thumb and finger. "It's pretty and it feels soft."

Becky turned around just enough to glimpse the fabric before turning away again. "I don't like it."

"*Oll recht*, there's plenty more to choose from. How about this one?" Mary nodded toward a bolt of deep purple fabric. "That's a lovely shade of purple, *ya*?"

Becky didn't turn around. "I don't like purple. It's an ugly color."

Mary looked down at the purple dress that she was wearing. "Purple's not so bad."

Becky spun around. "*Ya*, it is. I wouldn't be caught dead in it."

"That isn't very nice to say," Mary murmured. She thought she spoke too quietly for Becky to hear, but the girl pursed her lips and stalked off.

Mary closed her eyes and took a fortifying breath, then opened her eyes and braced herself to try again. She followed Becky past a shelf stocked with Singer sewing machines and caught up with her beside a rack of men's black winter hats. "Let's not give up, *ya*?" Mary said with a cheerful grin. "There's plenty of other colors to choose from here. What about emerald-green? Or pink?"

Becky spun around, her expression fierce. "If I can't have the turquoise, I don't want anything at all."

Mary froze.

"And why are you staring at me with that *narrisch* grin on your face? Why are you always smiling, when there's nothing to smile about?"

The smile died on Mary's face, replaced by a sinking humiliation. She could imagine what she must look like, trailing this petulant girl through the store, pleading with ridiculous smiles and placating words to be accepted. Betty's encouraging words rushed through her mind. So did Gabriel and Eliza's advice from earlier that week. And all the times over the years that Gabriel had quietly shaken his head and murmured, *Ach, Mary, I wish you could break free.*

She had not understood what he had meant until now. But as she stared at Becky's churlish expression, Mary suddenly did. And a need to stand up for herself whooshed through her body like a storm. She could never appease Becky enough to earn her love. Mary raised her chin and tightened her hands into fists until her fingernails pressed into her palms. "*Oll recht*. Then you won't get anything. We're going home now."

Becky balked. "But..."

Mary did not wait for Becky to protest. "If you don't *kumme* with me then you can find your own way home." She spun around and marched toward the door. A stab of guilt struck her as she passed Betty, who was waiting behind the counter to cut the fabric and ring them up. "I'm sorry," Mary said in a low voice. "We aren't getting anything today."

"Oh." Betty looked surprised, until she looked over at Becky, who stood watching them with her arms crossed and face red as she fought tears. Then she nodded slowly. "I see." Betty patted Mary on the arm. "Being a *mamm* isn't easy, especially to a *youngie* you've only just met. She'll *kumme* around." Betty winked and squeezed Mary's arm. "And in the meantime, keep standing your ground."

A renewed wave of strength gripped Mary. She held her head high as she walked out of the shop. But it didn't take long for her resolve to weaken again. Becky refused to speak on the ride home and Mary desperately wanted to say something to comfort her. But she did not. Instead, they traveled in silence. The only sound came from the hard, rhythmic clacking of her horse's hooves on the pavement and the whistle of a cold wind through the bare tree branches lining the road.

When Mary's house finally came into view, she heard a sniffle and cut her eyes to the side to see a fat tear slide down Becky's face. The girl wiped it away quickly and pulled her black winter cloak more tightly around her body.

"It's *oll recht* to cry," Mary said.

"I'm not crying."

Mary looked over and raised an eyebrow.

Becky sniffled again. "Okay. Maybe just a little."

"You've got a lot to be upset about." Mary considered her words carefully. She would rather sit quietly and pretend none of this was happening. Instead, she forced out her next sentence. "But that doesn't mean you can take it out on me or blame me for it. What have I done since you've been here but try to help you? I know you might not like me or the way I do things, but I've done nothing to hurt you."

Tears rushed from Becky's eyes. She sucked in a shuddering breath, then covered her face with her hands. "I just want to go home." A sob racked her thin body. "It wasn't really about the color of the dress. I just want to be back where everything feels right. Nothing is the same here."

"I know."

"Why did everything have to change?" The words sounded muffled behind Becky's hands.

Mary sighed as she considered her answer. "Because nothing can stay the same. But not all change is bad—even when it comes out of bad circumstances. *Gott* can take the fire and all the losses in your life and make something *gut* from it all."

"Do you really believe that?" Becky lowered her hands enough for her eyes to show so she could peek out at Mary.

"I do."

"How?"

Mary tugged on the reins to guide Red Rover into her driveway. The buggy clattered over the dip where the pavement met concrete. "*Vell*, for starters, I see the *gut* because I get to have you in my life. You and your *bruder* and your *daed*."

"Do you really want me in your life?"

"Of course, I do."

"Even though you're not my real *mamm*?"

"I didn't give birth to you, but that doesn't mean I can't be a real *mamm* to you, if you'll let me. Not all mothers are related to their *kinner* by blood. And they don't love those *kinner* any less than if they were."

Becky didn't say anything as the buggy rattled past the row of maple trees lining her front yard and stopped in front of the barn. Mary started to slide out of her seat to go open the barn door so she could drive the buggy inside, but Becky grabbed her arm. "I'm sorry. I shouldn't have taken things out on you. I know you were just trying to help."

Mary smiled. But this time it was genuine and not forced. "*Danki* for saying so. How about we start things over between us and try going back to the fabric shop tomorrow? I bet you'd look nice in pink."

Becky's tearstained face lit up. "Do you really mean that? You'll take me back and help me?"

"Sure. All I ask is that you treat me the way you want to be treated. *Oll recht?*"

Becky looked sheepish, but managed a small nod. *"Oll recht."*

The barn door creaked open and Silas appeared in the doorway. "I thought I heard you out here." He pushed the double doors all the way open to let them through. "Come on in and get warmed up. It's freezing out there."

"Walk on," Mary said as she flicked the reins. Becky's words had warmed her so much that she had forgotten to be cold. It felt so good to have Becky sitting beside her as Silas welcomed them home.

But as the buggy rumbled into the barn, Silas's expression shifted and Mary felt that familiar tightness in her belly return. "What's happened?" he asked as he stared at Becky. "Why is she crying?"

Mary swallowed hard. She didn't like that Silas was acting as if his daughter wasn't even there. "You should ask her. She can tell you better than I can."

"What have you done, Becky?" Silas asked.

"I haven't done anything!" Becky glanced from her father to Mary, then back to her father again. "I mean, maybe I did, but it wasn't anything that bad and it's *oll recht* now. We talked about it and—"

"I knew I shouldn't have let you go," Silas interrupted.

"Why do you always think I'm doing something wrong? Maybe I'm just upset!"

"You just said you did something, but that it's *oll recht* now. Did you or didn't you do something?"

"You're making it impossible to explain, *Daed*!"

Silas threw up his hands in frustration. "When Mary told me she wanted to take you to town, I thought it was a bad idea. I knew you'd get into some kind of trouble."

"Why would you assume that about me? It isn't fair!"

"Didn't you get into trouble back home, running with the wrong crowd of *youngies*?"

Becky looked down, her face tight. "Nothing too bad."

"Bad enough." Silas shook his head. "I'm not going to argue with you. Get inside and get supper started. You know your way around Mary's kitchen by now. Don't go hide in your room and be idle. There's been enough of that."

Becky opened her mouth to protest, but the look on Silas's face silenced her. She tumbled out of the buggy and raced out of the barn, her footsteps echoing in the strained silence.

Chapter Six

Silas looked at Mary's face and wanted to sink into the floor. He hadn't meant for the conversation to end with Becky running away and Mary looking at him with disappointment. He couldn't seem to live up to his new wife's expectations. And the worst part was, those expectations were completely reasonable. He owed her much more than he was giving her.

But how could he explain his fears to Mary? He would have to admit to everything in his past. And then, what if Mary blamed him? What would happen when she learned that he had failed to keep his first wife safe? What if she believed that he could not keep her safe, either?

All Silas wanted was to keep his family safe—Becky, Ethan, and now Mary. That realization sent a ripple of purpose through him. Yes. Mary was his family now and he felt a fierce need to protect her. How could he not? She was so sweet and caring, so full of love. She deserved someone to stand with her, to take up for her. He wanted to be that person.

But how could he do that without risking more hurt for both of them? He would have to be careful, to keep his distance while still trying to help her.

He approached the buggy, even though everything in him shouted to run away and hide, instead of facing his shame. "I'll take care of Red Rover," he said, more gruffly than he had intended. The frustration was still running through his veins. He forced the frown off his face, hoped he didn't look upset. "I mean, I'd like to help with the horse so you can relax." This time, his tone was gentler.

Mary climbed out of the buggy without a word. Silas took hold of Red Rover's halter and made sure to keep his voice soft. "Hello, big guy. Ready for some oats and a warm stall?" He patted the horse's flank, but his attention was on Mary. She hovered beside the buggy, biting her bottom lip. "What is it?" he asked.

She shook her head.

He exhaled. "I'm sorry. I didn't mean..." He shook his head. "Why are you looking at me like that?"

"Because you're speaking to the horse with more understanding than you give your own *dochder*."

Silas flinched. He knew she was right. He exhaled again and ran his fingers through his hair. "Can you forgive me?" Somehow, the harder he tried, the more he failed. And he had no one to blame but himself. Maybe it was time to soften those walls around him.

No. Everything inside him might collapse if he let those walls come down. How would he take care of his family then?

Mary didn't speak for a moment and Silas dreaded her answer. His pulse thudded in his ears as he studied her calm but distant expression.

"Becky's the one you need to be asking, not me," she said finally. He saw a flicker of anxiety pass over her face and he realized how much that statement had cost her.

He responded with a grim nod. "You're right."

Her eyes widened. "You admit it? Just like that?"

Silas shrugged. "Did you expect a fight? If I'm wrong, I admit when I'm wrong."

"I, uh… I guess I did. In my experience…" She shook her head and looked away.

His chest tightened at her words. It had only taken one, short conversation with Mary's brother to give Silas a good idea of what she had been through. And Silas knew that pain inflicted by loved ones hurt more deeply than any other.

There was so much he wanted to say, but he didn't know where to begin. "I'll make it right with Becky. I didn't mean to come down on her so hard."

"I can see that you're trying to reach her, that you're..." She looked up at him to judge his reaction. "Afraid for her."

"How could you tell?"

Mary folded her hands in front of her and studied them as she spoke. "My *daed* didn't care about reaching me. He only cared about getting his own way. So I know the difference."

Silas stepped closer to her. After meeting Elmo, he had suspected that her father had hurt her too. That was a wound that would last a lifetime. She looked so frail and hurt, standing there in the flickering light of the kerosene lantern hanging on the wall beside her. He wanted to pull her into his arms and whisper that everything would be okay from now on. "I'm sorry, Mary."

"It's *oll recht*."

"I don't think it is."

"*Nee*, I don't suppose so."

Silas took another step toward her. He could hear Red Rover's breath beside him and the creak of wood settling into place as the sun went down and the temperature dropped. "I wish I could take the hurt away."

Mary gave a sad little smile. "Maybe you can." But her eyes looked skeptical.

Silas realized he had said too much. He was tiptoeing into dangerous territory, where his heart took over for his mind. He cleared his throat and broke eye contact. "I should get Red Rover in his stall."

"*Ya.*" Mary turned away, then stopped and turned back to face him. "But you'll speak to Becky?"

Silas nodded. "I'll try."

"That's all any of us can do."

Silas watched Mary walk away, and a

cold, empty feeling settled inside of him. For the first time, he wondered if he was doing the right thing to push her away. She was kind and wise, and he knew that she could help his family, if only he would let her.

More than that, he longed to connect with her over more than just his daughter. He saw that Mary had a hidden world inside of her that she kept tightly under wraps. What a privilege it would be to hear her secret thoughts, to sit under the stars and talk about their dreams and hopes together. Mary was far more lovely and complex than he had ever imagined she could be.

Then he reminded himself that his first wife had been lovely and complex, too. Before their marriage turned into a maze of secrets and lies that pushed them apart forever. He would never allow that to happen again.

Mary considered everything that Silas had said to her. She replayed the conversation over and over as she tossed and turned beneath her quilt that night. The next morning, she could not stop thinking of him as she dressed in the early morning chill. The floorboards were cold against her bare feet and she quickly pulled on her black stockings, then arranged her hair in a tight, braided bun, slipped into her everyday work dress and fastened her starched white *kapp* into place on her head.

What if he had taken what she'd said the wrong way yesterday? Did he think she was against him? She had only wanted to help his relationship with his daughter. But he had seemed so distant and unreachable when she had finally found the courage to confront him.

Mary did the only thing she knew how to do in a situation like this. She prepared a huge breakfast to prove to him that she cared. She had done the same thing for her father and brother when they used to ignore her. She had always thought that if she just tried a little bit harder, they would appreciate her and respond to her love.

The kitchen had been bathed in darkness when she began to cook. By the time she was finished, sunlight flooded the room and the sound of car engines drifted up from the street. She blew out the kerosene lantern, stretched her back and sighed. She could only hope her efforts were good enough.

When Silas did not appear for breakfast, she tiptoed upstairs and saw that the door to his room was open and his bed was neatly made. She could not have tucked in the corners of the sheets any better herself. How nice it was to have a husband who looked after himself, instead of expecting her to follow him around like a child and straighten the mess he left behind. It did feel strange, though, or unfamiliar at least. And it made her a little uncomfortable. What value could she bring if she couldn't take care of the house for him? She and her mother had always taken care of every detail for her father and brother. She could not imagine them making their own beds or pouring their own coffee. Not when they had other people to do it for them. Sure, they never really acknowledged her or her mother's efforts, but doing all that work had made Mary feel like she had some kind of control, some way to earn their affection and approval.

How could she win over Silas if he already took care of himself?

Mary doubled back to the kitchen, heaped a plate full of sausage-and-egg casserole, biscuits, gravy, hash-brown casserole and a slice of cold apple pie, then covered it with tinfoil. She poured freshly brewed, black coffee into a thermos, sealed the lid, slipped into her heavy winter cloak and headed out into the frosty morning air.

Silas looked up from sawing a length of lumber when she pushed open the barn door. She had hoped for a smile, but instead he looked concerned. "What have you got there?" he asked.

Mary closed the door behind her and stepped into the warmth of the barn. Red Rover's body heat and the propane heater kept the space snug enough that Silas had removed his coat and hung it over a sawhorse. "Breakfast and *kaffi*. But I can bring it back to the kitchen if you don't want it." Mary felt a sinking sensation in her stomach.

"*Nee*, of course, I want it. *Danki*, Mary." Silas set down the handsaw and wiped his forehead with his sleeve. "It's just that you didn't need to go to all the trouble. I can help myself to what you've made. You don't have to *kumme* out in the cold to bring it to me."

"It's no trouble."

Silas looked at her for a moment, as if choosing his words carefully. Then he smiled, but his eyes looked sad. "*Vell, danki*. For sure and certain I appreciate it." She handed him the plate and he peeled back the tinfoil. His smile dropped into a frown. "Mary, this is another feast. You didn't have to do this. You must have spent all morning cooking."

"*Ach*, it's nothing."

Silas's eyes glanced up from the plate and locked on hers. "It isn't nothing, Mary. It's a lot of effort and I appreciate it."

"Oh." Silas's words, and the look of respect in his eyes, sent a wave of happiness through her body. She was not used to being appreciated and it felt so good she wanted to waltz out of the barn singing.

Mary spent the rest of the day cooking and cleaning and trying to guess exactly what Silas was thinking and feeling. She wanted to ask him outright instead of imagining, but was too afraid of what he might say. So she tried her best to guess at what would make him happy. But the more she did for him, the more he frowned.

Mary tried to ignore how his frowns made her feel and focused on getting her family a new wardrobe to replace what had been lost in the fire. She dropped in on a few close friends to organize a sewing frolic, and took Becky back to Beiler's

Quilt and Fabric Shop. This time, Becky chatted happily and thanked Mary for helping her pick out the right fabrics. Betty winked at Mary from across the store and gave a knowing smile. Mary felt a growing excitement inside her. Becky had begun to soften toward her, even if only a little.

The more she saw Becky soften, the more Mary recognized that the accommodating kind of love she had been giving her stepdaughter had not been love at all. Love was more nuanced than that. Love required a person to set boundaries and to expect respect in return. Mary knew she had found the right balance with Becky, but she recognized she was still missing it with Silas. Why shouldn't she expect his love and respect? Something deep inside told her that she should. But as quick as that realization came, she tamped it down again. She didn't know how to let go of old expectations that were as familiar to her as breathing.

But she'd keep trying to…

* * *

Arleta Kauffman, Sadie Lapp, Eliza King and Viola Esch—who managed to secure an invite to nearly every church district activity—arrived the next day armed with sewing baskets and several plates of freshly baked chocolate-chip cookies. "It's so *gut* to see you getting out," Mary said to Arleta and embraced her in a tight hug.

"Ach, oll recht." Arleta patted Mary's back and pulled back from the hug as fast as she could. "I appreciate the warm *willkumm*, but that doesn't make me a hugger."

Mary didn't feel rejected because she knew Arleta's personality and that she loved her friends, despite keeping her distance. Instead, Mary laughed, and her friends joined in. "*Gut* to see you're back to being your old self."

Arleta waved her away. "*Ya*, *vell*, I've had a lot of help."

Sadie, who had recently married Arleta's brother, had been a tremendous support during Arleta's long rehabilitation after the buggy accident. Sadie beamed and her rosy cheeks turned a deeper shade of red. She seemed embarrassed by the attention, but Mary was glad Sadie was getting the thanks she deserved. The Kauffman family had been completely transformed since she had married Vernon and become a stepmother to his children.

"Where's the new husband?" Viola asked, cutting into the conversation. A second round of laughter passed through the living room.

"You're getting straight to the point," Eliza said as she sat down in one of the wooden rocking chairs and began to rummage through her sewing basket.

"Same as you do, Eliza."

Eliza gave a sly smile as she pulled out her needle and thread. "Fair enough."

"So, where is he?" Viola repeated. She hobbled across the room, her cane thumping against the hard wood floor, and took the upholstered armchair.

Mary felt suddenly self-conscious. "In

the barn. His *kinner* are out there helping him set up the harness shop. Becky will *kumme* back to help us sew in a few minutes."

"Mary, you're blushing," Eliza said and raised her eyebrows.

"Young love," Viola said with a grin.

"I'm hardly young," Mary said. "And we're not… I mean…"

"*Ach*, you're plenty young," Viola said. "Oh, to be in my thirties again!" She snorted. "It would be nice just to be in my sixties again."

"*Oll recht*. I'm still young, I guess. But about the other thing… We're not…"

"You're not what?" Viola leaned forward. "Get it out, why don't you?"

"Viola," Arleta chided. "Leave her alone. Can't you see the marriage is failing."

"What? *Nee!* It's not failing." Mary suddenly regretted inviting them all over at the same time. She loved her friends dearly, but they were all very blunt. Only

Sadie knew how to hold back her words, and Mary looked to her for help.

Sadie smiled when Mary caught her eye. "She never said the marriage is failing. These things just take time, is all. You know, I barely knew Vernon when I went to work as a nanny for him. He was a hard man to read. We had nothing in common and I was convinced he didn't like me. Next thing you know we were getting married." She flashed her signature grin.

"Gabriel and I are complete opposites," Eliza said. "No one thought we would ever get together—especially me." She pushed her big, round glasses up the bridge of her nose. "And look at us now."

"*Ya*, but..." Mary ran her fingers along a bolt of pink cloth lying on the folding table she had set up for the work frolic. "I'm not sure Silas and I are so different, actually."

"Then what's the problem?" Viola asked.

"I never said there was one."

"We weren't born yesterday," Viola said. She rolled her eyes. "Especially me."

The other women chuckled.

Sadie looked at Mary, then reached over and squeezed her arm. "You don't have to talk about it if you don't want to, but it might help if you do."

Mary exhaled. "I don't know what to say. Silas doesn't like me very much, that's all. *Vell*, sometimes I think we're starting to connect, but then..." She shook her head and pushed the bolt of fabric away. "Never mind. I shouldn't expect him to fall in love with me. That's silly. He didn't marry me for all that nonsense."

"*Ach*, Mary." Sadie's blue eyes looked sad. "It's *oll recht* to want to be loved and to love someone back in return. Who wouldn't want that?"

Mary hesitated, then blurted out, "That's easy for you to say, Sadie. You've got plenty to offer. Who wouldn't fall in love with you? You're beautiful, a talented artist, sweet-natured and always cheerful. You can expect to be loved."

Sadie leaned back, as if struck just

then. She took a moment to compose her thoughts. "I see how it might seem that way. But I've actually spent most of my life feeling like an outsider within my own community. I've felt my share of rejection."

Mary's mouth dropped open. "You have?"

"*Ya.* I'm an Amish artist. That's a controversial combination for certain sure."

"But you're so talented. You even get to sell your work at Aunt Fannie's Amish Gift Shop. You've been helping the Kauffmans through your art therapy."

"*Ya*, and I nearly got shunned for it."

Arleta clucked her tongue. "That's all in the past. We've dealt with it. She knows she's accepted now." Arleta looked up from the needle she was threading. "Don't you?"

Sadie gave her a sly grin. "*Ya.* I know you love me, even if you don't admit it."

"*Ach.*" Arleta waved her sister-in-law away, but couldn't suppress a small smile. "No need to talk about it."

Mary chuckled. Arleta had become a close friend of Sadie's, though she would never admit it out loud.

The sound of Viola's cane hitting the floor startled everyone and their attention shot to the elderly woman. "You've all forgotten what we were talking about." She motioned toward Mary with a thin, bony finger. "Mary here doesn't think she's worth loving."

"*Nee*, I didn't say that." Mary picked up the metal sewing scissors from the folding table. "Not exactly."

Viola heaved a long-suffering sigh. "You didn't have to."

"I can think of a million reasons to love you, Mary," Sadie said. Her brow crinkled. "I love you for just being you, but there are so many things that I like about you. Let's see, you are always reading and you always have something interesting to say about what you've read. And you're really smart. You see things other people don't. I always like hearing what you have to say, Mary."

"You do?"

"Of course."

Mary stood frozen. She had no idea how to react to that. It was too surprising.

"And your nephew loves you to pieces," Eliza said. "Gabriel sees you as a mother and a best friend, rolled into one."

A smile tugged at Mary's lips. "That's nice to say, Eliza."

"You know me," Eliza said. "I only say things if they're true, whether people like it or not."

"That's for certain sure," Mary said.

Viola hit the floor with the end of her cane to regain their attention. "Your father's been gone a long time, Mary. It's time you laid those hurts to rest."

Mary felt a rush of emotion wash over her. She turned away, too exposed by Viola's words. "I should go get Becky so we can start sewing."

"Not until we finish the conversation.

Stop changing the topic and ignoring the facts."

"I'm not—"

"Becky had an outburst at your wedding reception," Viola interrupted. "And then another one at Beiler's Quilt and Fabric Shop."

"How did you know—"

"Betty and I talk. Do you think that silly Sew-N-Save could tempt me away from a *gut* Amish shop?"

"Right. I see."

"Betty also said that Becky seemed to be doing better the second time she came into the shop."

Mary swallowed hard. Viola was not going to let up.

"So, is she doing better?"

Mary looked down and traced a crack in the table with her finger. "I think she's starting to adjust a little. Or I hope so, anyway."

"Do you know what's helping her?"

"*Ach*, I don't know…"

"You stopped letting her walk all over you, that's what," Viola said.

Mary shrugged sheepishly.

"You need to keep standing up for yourself—with *everyone*."

"Wait." Eliza stiffened in her chair. "Silas isn't mistreating you, is he? I mean, is there something you need to stand up to him about?" Her eyes cut to Viola. "Is there something you know that I don't?"

"A lot, I'm sure," Viola said with a sly smile.

Eliza rolled her eyes but returned the smile.

"But, *nee*, he isn't mistreating her, as far as I know." Viola directed her attention at Mary. "Is he?"

All the women stared at Mary until she felt her cheeks burning. "*Nee, nee*. Not at all. He's just distant. I can't seem to get through to him. But he's a kind man. There's some conflict between him and Becky, but he's working on being more understanding, I think. It seems like he's just afraid." Mary clamped her mouth shut. She hadn't meant to say anything so personal about Silas.

"He's not the only one," Arleta said.

Mary frowned.

"Arleta's right," Eliza said. "I think you're both afraid of each other. Trusting someone to love you isn't easy."

"Afraid of each other?" Mary set down the scissors with a thump. "*Vell*, now, that's just silly."

All three of her friends gave her a look that said otherwise.

"You know," Eliza began, "you could try talking to him instead of whatever it is you're doing now to earn his love."

"I never said I'm trying to earn his love."

"I know you well enough to know how you think, Mary. You don't love yourself enough to believe you deserve anyone else's love. That's why we're here today. We want you to see otherwise."

"What do you mean? I thought you were here to sew!"

"We're here for both," Arleta said dryly. "And I'm starting to get one of my headaches. So I'm going to cut to the chase. You've got plenty to offer. Believe that and stop trying to earn Silas's love. He'll come around and recognize your value."

"But how?"

Arleta shook her head and set down her needle. "Oh, Mary. How could he not?"

Mary felt hot and exposed. Everyone knew how she felt. Her instinct was to run to her room, slam the door shut and hide beneath her quilt.

But another part of her felt free. She liked what her friends were saying about her, even if they were a little too direct about it. Her spine felt a little straighter, her heart a little lighter. She wanted to believe their words. She wanted to accept herself for who she was.

But could she trust that Silas would too?

Chapter Seven

Silas was touched that Mary had organized a sewing frolic for him and his children. It felt good to finally have a change of clothes that fit him well. Now, he was excited to show her what he had been working on for her and their family. He noticed that he had started thinking of them all as one family, not strangers trying to find a way to live together. Funny how he and Mary had found a simple rhythm with one another, even though they had only been married for six days. Somehow, it just felt right.

"Kumme," Silas said to everyone as he

pushed back his chair and stood up. “Now that we’ve finished supper, I have something to show you all.”

“What is it, *Daed*?” Ethan leaped up from his seat at the table.

Becky stood up slowly, making a point not to show too much interest, but Silas caught the flicker of curiosity on her face and smiled. Mary was busy carrying dishes from the table to the sink. He gently grabbed her arm as she strode past him. “Won’t you *kumme*, too, please?”

She looked startled, but returned his smile. “As soon as I finish the dishes. I can’t leave them.”

“*Ach*, I think you can.”

“Come on, Mary!” Ethan crowded between them. “You have to *kumme* with us.”

“Just as soon as I finish.”

“Nope.” Silas shook his head, a smile still on his face. “We’ll all help when we’re finished. Will that convince you?”

“*Nee*, you don’t need to—”

"I insist." Silas eased the stack of dishes from her hands and set them back on the table, while Ethan tugged her by the sleeve toward the living room.

They were hurrying through the brisk night air a moment later. "I'll race you," Ethan shouted as he took off across the yard. Silas shot after him, dodging a maple tree to cut Ethan off before he crossed the driveway.

"Let's go!" Mary shouted Becky. Then Silas heard their footsteps pounding behind him.

He reached the barn door first, slamming into it at nearly full speed with a booming thud. Ethan made it a few paces behind. "Second place!" he shouted as he slapped the barn wall. Silas turned to watch Mary and Becky flying across the lawn, the skirts of their dresses hitched up and their faces glowing. He had not seen Mary look so carefree before. It suited her. He couldn't help but admire her simple, unconventional beauty as she grinned beneath the moonlight, laughing out loud, her eyes fierce with competition as she overtook Becky. They hit the barn wall with a sharp bang at nearly the same time, breathing hard. Mary bent forward and braced her hands on her knees as she caught her breath.

"Who won?" Becky asked.

"I think it was a tie," Ethan said.

"I didn't know you could race like that, Mary," Silas said. "You could run track if you were an *Englischer*." He was teasing but Mary glanced at him with embarrassment in her eyes.

She straightened up and shook her head. "I got carried away. It's *hochmut* to want to win like that. I'm sorry. I can get competitive if I'm not careful."

Silas frowned. He wanted to make Mary understand that she didn't have to keep trying to be good enough. Nothing she ever did would fill that need that was eating her away inside. It was a bottomless pit. His late wife had had her own bottomless pit. She had filled it with drinking and risk-taking, until she destroyed herself. He realized that Mary filled the need inside of her in her own way. He had to help her break free from that prison, even though a little voice inside warned him that he shouldn't get involved. After all, no matter how hard he tried, he had never been able to help Linda.

He sighed and scratched his beard. Something had to be said, despite his reservations. "Mary, I don't think it's prideful to have fun with your family. You didn't do anything wrong. Besides, I did it, too."

"I didn't mean to imply that you did anything wrong!"

"I know you didn't."

Mary's forehead creased as she listened.

"I meant that…it's *oll recht* to just have a little fun. That's all. There was nothing more to it."

Mary looked slightly confused, then surprised. A genuine smile overtook her.

Silas saw that she was not used to healthy, straightforward communication. She had been expecting his reassurance to be a trap. His muscles tightened at the thought of what her family must have put her through to steal her ability to relax and enjoy the moment.

"We did have fun, didn't we?" she said with a sheepish grin.

"Ya." Silas slid his arm in hers. "We did." He turned to look at her. She was close enough that he could smell her lavender soap and feel the warmth of her body through her black winter cloak. "And you look beautiful when you smile like that. You should do it more often."

Mary's eyes widened as she stared in his. Then her cheeks flushed red and she looked down. "That's nice to hear, Silas," she murmured so softly that he could barely hear. *"Danki."*

"Now," he said as he pulled her a fraction closer. "Look what I've done in here."

Silas pushed open the barn door to reveal the new harness shop, with everything set up and ready for business. The shelves that he had built with Mary's old lumber stood in a neat row, gleaming with wood varnish and stocked with supplies. Three tables were arranged in front of the shelves, each one covered with the equipment that Silas used to make leather harnesses and other tack. Red Rover's stall stood against the opposite wall, alongside neatly stacked feedbags and bales of hay. The horse stomped a hoof and snorted at the sudden commotion.

Mary clapped her hands together. "It's *wunderbar*, Silas!" She surveyed the transformed space as she breathed in deeply. "And it smells so *gut*, too." The scent of leather and fresh-cut wood filled the air. "I can't believe how you've remade the barn into a workshop. It's like a different place entirely."

Silas felt a warm glow at Mary's praise. He had not realized how much her approval meant to him. It felt good to know that she appreciated his efforts. He realized that feeling was the same one that Mary was chasing every day. Everyone was, he supposed. But for people like Mary, who had been told over and over that they weren't good enough, it was harder to believe that feeling. He wondered what he could do to show her that she was appreciated.

"Look at this," Mary said as she wandered over to his equipment. "It's so much like the Singer sewing machines at the fabric shop." She bent down, getting to eye level with the details, then stood up and chuckled.

"*Ya*. It is." He watched as she studied the machine with interest. "Would you like to try it? It's kind of like sewing a dress, I suppose, but with different materials."

"*Ach, nee*. I couldn't possibly." Mary quickly backed away from the machine.

"Why not?"

"I'd make a mistake. I wouldn't want to mess anything up."

"Mary, you ought to give yourself more credit."

Mary hesitated. "Wouldn't you rather I stay out of your way?"

Silas scratched his beard. A few days ago, he might have said yes. But after getting to know her, he could see that she was nothing like Linda. Mary seemed steady and calm, competent and determined. But how could he be sure? Maybe he shouldn't trust his impression of her.

He shifted his weight from one foot to the other. Working with Mary in the shop would make her a business partner, not a romantic one. He could still keep his distance where it mattered. He ignored the part of him that felt excited about the prospect of spending time with her. He would keep this strictly business.

"You're frowning. I should go. I need to finish up in the kitchen, anyway. I can see that you don't want me to interfere—"

"*Nee*, I was just thinking. I always frown when I think."

Mary hesitated. "What were you thinking?"

"That it would be nice to have your help. You seem interested in the equipment."

"Vell, ya." Mary looked down at her hands. "My *daed* used to work with farm

machinery—all gas-powered, of course—and it fascinated me. I like to take things apart to see how they work." She ran a finger along the side of the industrial sewing machine. "It's silly, I suppose."

"You like working with machinery?" The thought had never occurred to him, but why shouldn't she like it? He liked machinery, too.

"*Ya*. Like I said, it's silly of me."

"Silly? Not at all. Now you have to try."

"*Ach*, I don't know..."

But Silas could see the excitement in her eyes.

"Go on, Mary."

"*Ya!*" Ethan shouted. "We want to see you do *Daed*'s job!"

"Oh. *Nee*, that wouldn't be right." She shook her head and backed away from the machine. "What would the bishop and the elders have to say about me doing men's work?"

Silas shrugged. "I've never heard of an *Ordnung* that said a woman couldn't sew."

"*Nee*, but..." She looked up at Silas with a confused smile.

"C'mon, Mary." He nodded toward the sewing machine.

Mary pressed her hands to her cheeks as her smile widened into a grin. "*Ach, oll recht*. I'll give it a try."

"*Gut*. It operates a lot like a foot-powered treadle sewing machine. You'll get the hang of it pretty fast."

"But this isn't foot-powered." Her eyes moved to the motor in the corner of the barn. "Diesel-powered engine?"

"Ya." Silas glanced at his children and raised an eyebrow. "She's smart, ain't so?"

Mary studied the pulley connected to the engine. "So it's attached by a line shaft to turn the treadle."

Silas's eyes cut to Mary and he looked at her with admiration. "*Ya*. How'd you know about line shafts?"

She smiled. "I told you, I like machinery. I've never had a chance to do much with it, though. But I've read a lot about it and I used to watch my *daed* work, even though he never let me touch the equipment."

"*Vell*, you can use any of the equipment in my shop anytime you want. I won't stop you, that's for certain sure." Silas felt a surge of excitement at being able to make Mary happy in such an unexpected way. He realized that he wanted to make up for all the times her father kept her from doing what fulfilled her.

She looked up at him with shining eyes. "Really?"

"Really." Their gaze locked and Silas felt the connection between them. "Becky, Ethan, go on back to the house and clean the kitchen. Give Mary a chance to try out all the equipment and take a look at the motor."

"Fine with me," Becky said. "Motors are boring."

"*Ya*, she's kind of right," Ethan said. "But I still want to work with you when I grow up, *Daed*."

Silas patted his son on the back. "Making harnesses is about craftmanship more than anything else, so you don't have to like motors." He nodded over to Mary, who was busy examining the diesel engine. "Especially now that we've got Mary to take care of the equipment."

She straightened up. "Me…take care of the equipment?"

"Can we have pie after we clean the kitchen?" Ethan asked before Silas could answer Mary.

"Sure, why not?" Silas said. "To celebrate reopening the shop, *ya*?"

"Ya!" Ethan spun around and began running for the door. "I'll race you, Becky! You're too slow to catch up with me!"

"That's what you think!" Becky shouted as she hitched up her dress and sprinted after him.

Silas turned back to Mary. She had crouched back down, and was studying the hand clutch of the motor. "So, as I was saying, why shouldn't you take care of the equipment if you enjoy doing that?"

Mary stood up and frowned, her expression hardening. "I ought to get back to the house. You'll be wanting your after-supper cup of *kaffi*. I know you like that around this time of night."

"Stay," he said gently and reached for her hand.

She was silent as he wrapped his fingers around hers. Her hand felt warm and soft in his. It felt right.

But then, Mary shook her head and pulled her hand away. "*Nee*, you need your *kaffi*. I can't do men's work out here in the barn. It isn't right. What would people think?" She turned away. "What would *you* think?"

"I already told you what I think. I want you here, with me, doing what interests you."

She looked skeptical, as though his words were a trap.

"Mary, I never asked you to bring me *kaffi* and cookies all the time." He shook his head. "I don't even want you to." He hoped the frustration in his voice didn't show. Mary seemed like a deer in the forest, ready to bolt at any moment.

The color drained from Mary's face. "I don't understand. Don't you like what I do for you? If it's not *gut* enough…" Her voice trailed away.

"I didn't marry you to get a maid!" he said, more forcefully than he meant.

"Then why did you marry me?"

"Do you honestly believe that's all marriage is? Some kind of arrangement where the woman cooks and cleans all day and the man provides, and everyone's happy?"

"That's all you've shown me that you wanted. You said it yourself, on the day we married."

Silas clenched his jaw in frustration. He *had* said something to that effect. He tried to remember what he had told her exactly. Something about their marriage only ever being a business arrangement. What had he been thinking? He had tried to put up walls to protect them both, but that had been thoughtless. No wonder Mary was working day and night to earn his affection. He had made it sound like that was all he wanted from her. He couldn't believe how inconsiderate he had been. It was inexcusable, even though his intentions had been good. But intentions weren't what mattered. Words and actions were.

Mary pulled away and hurried across the barn, clutching her black cloak tightly around her chest. Silas realized that he must have looked angry, staring down at her. But the only person he was angry with was himself. He had tried so hard to protect Mary from his past, but had only ended up hurting her instead. "Mary, wait!" He jogged after her. "I'm so sorry. I didn't mean to hurt you."

Mary stuttered to a stop at the barn door, but did not turn around. She was trembling. "Don't you see?" she whispered. "How will you ever learn to love me if you don't let me bring you *kaffi* or make your bed or cook you big meals?" She braced her forearm against the door and pressed her face into the crook of her elbow to smother a sob. "What more can I do?"

"Mary." He began to speak gently as he

placed a hand on her shoulder. "You've got it all wrong." He hesitated. The truth was burning inside of him, shouting to be released. But if he said everything he felt, he would never be the same. It would be like throwing himself off a cliff, with no way of knowing where he would land. He swallowed hard. He could not tell her how deep his feelings for her had become. But he could still tell her something. "I appreciate you for you. Not for what you do for me. I mean, I do appreciate how hard you work for the *kinner* and me. Sure, I enjoy your cooking, and it's nice to have a clean, organized home, especially after having to do most of that myself over the years, while raising the *kinner* alone. But you know what I enjoy more?"

After a few beats, Mary lifted her face from the crook of her elbow and turned around. "What?" she asked in a ragged voice.

His heart ached at the sight of her tear-stained face. Before he could stop himself, he lifted a finger and gently wiped a tear from her cheek. "I enjoy talking to you. Hearing your thoughts and your perspective on the world. I enjoy seeing you get excited about your interests—like you did about the machinery. I like the thought of us working together in the shop—*our* shop." He gave her a bashful smile and wiped another tear from her cheek. "Maybe you can teach me something about diesel engines, *ya*?"

"I don't understand. I thought you just wanted this to be a business arrangement."

Silas stopped and considered his words. Staring down into her dark gray eyes, all he could think about was how much he wanted to spend his days with her because being with her made him happy. But he held back. "*Vell*, the harness shop is a business…"

"Oh." She gave a soft little chuckle. "*Ya*, I guess that makes sense."

Silas wanted to say so much more. Instead, he sighed and hoped he could get through to her, while still holding back. "Do you understand now, Mary? You're worth so much more than you realize. You don't have to prove anything to me."

She shook her head. "I don't know what to say."

"How about that you believe me?"

"Oll recht." Her smile was so pure and real that it sent a wave of warmth through Silas that he had never felt before. "I believe you."

All of his hopes and fears were colliding—and hope was winning. He could sense it building in him with every encounter that he had with Mary. He had planned for a safe, distant marriage of convenience.

Instead, he had found a woman who made him feel alive for the first time in years.

Chapter Eight

You're worth so much more than you realize. Silas's words filled Mary's heart and echoed in her mind. She thought about them as she fell asleep that night, snug and warm beneath her quilt. And they were the first thing on her mind when her bare feet hit the cold floorboards the next morning. She headed downstairs with an extra bounce in her step. Today, she would see if Silas really meant what he said.

Mary threw together a quick breakfast of oatmeal and raisins—with no eggs or bacon or anything else to go along with it, which felt scandalous—then delegated household chores to Becky before hurrying to the barn.

"You mean you trust me to take care of the house on my own?" Becky's eyes looked hopeful.

"I certain sure do."

Becky's face lit up. "Can I do the meal planning too? I like to decide what we eat."

"Sure."

"I don't want to do all the laundry on my own, though."

Mary laughed. "Nobody does. Don't worry. I'm hoping to spend more of my time helping your *daed* in his workshop from now on, but I'll still be doing some of the housework too."

"Sounds *gut*. As long as I get to take over the kitchen." A new confidence sparkled in Becky's eyes.

Mary grinned. "It's all yours, if you want it."

"I certain sure do." Becky grinned as she slipped into a fresh apron. "I hope you like lasagna because we'll be having a lot of it from now on. That's my favorite."

"Whatever you want. It's your choice, now."

Becky's face flashed with satisfaction as she reached for the cookbook on the kitchen counter. Mary's plan was off to a perfect start. She had been right to suspect that Becky craved the reassurance that comes from being trusted with more responsibility.

Mary and Silas spent the day side by side as he showed her how to use the machinery and walked her through the process of crafting a leather harness. Ethan delighted in watching Mary get the hang of using the industrial sewing machine. "*Gut* job, Mary," he proclaimed in his most serious voice as he leaned over her to examine her row of stitches. "You catch on fast." Mary and Silas exchanged an amused glance and chuckled at how Ethan was acting like a teacher, rather than an apprentice.

"It's *gut* to see him settling in," Mary whispered to Silas when Ethan crossed the room to fetch an awl. "He's so much more talkative than he was when you first arrived. It's hard to believe that was only one week ago."

Silas watched his son rifle through the supply shelf. "*Ya.* He's coming out of his shell. You've been *gut* for him, Mary. He's needed the comfort and support that you've given him." Silas ran his fingers through his hair. "I, uh, *vell*, I don't know what to say but thank you."

Mary could not believe was what happening. Somehow, her harebrained marriage scheme was transforming into a family. She turned to Silas with shining eyes. "I'm so pleased that he's happy here." She remembered the shy little boy who had arrived at her home so recently. Sure, he was still frail and often unsure of himself, but he had come such a long way already. "I think he's ready to start school. He looks so confident compared to just a few days ago."

Silas frowned. "*Ach*, I don't know about that."

Mary shifted her gaze from Ethan to Silas. She had expected him to be eager and relieved at the thought of Ethan returning to school, but instead his mouth was drawn into a tight line. "But why not? He needs to meet more *kinner* his age. And the longer he waits, the harder it will be for him to adjust, ain't so?"

Silas studied Ethan with that hard expression, then turned back to his worktable. "I ought to get started on the order the Yoders put in. They're my first customer in Bluebird Hills and I want to make a good impression."

"But…" Mary didn't finish her thought. Instead, she was interrupted by Becky walking into the barn with sandwiches.

"Lunchtime," Becky announced as she set the tray on one of the worktables.

"Danki," Mary said. "This looks *abbeditlich*. You'll stay and eat with us?"

Becky gave her a shy glance as she passed out the sandwiches. "*Ya*. I brought my sandwich out here, too, if you don't mind..."

"*Kumme* sit by me and let's talk about where we should go tomorrow," Mary said to her. "It's a visiting Sunday you know, and it's time you began to meet some *youngies* in the district."

Silas's frown deepened as he observed their conversation in silence. But Mary barely noticed his disapproval. She was too excited that Becky wanted to spend time with her.

"Are you looking forward to making new friends?" Mary asked as Becky passed out the sandwiches.

"Ya." Becky pushed a stray lock of hair beneath her *kapp* and looked down. "I just hope I fit in."

"You certain sure will!" Mary said and squeezed her arm. She leaned closer and winked. "You might even meet a nice young man, ain't so?"

Silas cleared his throat. "No need for all

that." His eyes stayed on his sandwich, but the concern was clearly etched on his face.

"Why not?" Mary asked.

Silas took a bite of his sandwich and chewed. They waited in silence. He shrugged and swallowed. "Better to be safe."

"I don't understand," Mary said.

"*Daed* doesn't trust me," Becky said. She glared at her father, but there was more pain than anger behind her eyes.

"*Nee*, it's not that…exactly." Silas set down his sandwich and shifted in his chair. "It's easy to make bad choices at your age, easy to fall into trouble. Can't be too careful, ain't so?"

"There's a difference in being careful and keeping me from courting."

"I married too young and I don't want you to make the same mistake. I thought—" Silas shook his head. "Never mind. I'm sorry. I shouldn't have said anything." He stood up abruptly.

"It's *oll recht*, Silas," Mary said. "It's

best to explain these things. Otherwise, how can we understand where you're coming from?"

Silas hesitated for a moment, then shook his head. "I need to get back to work."

Mary wanted to know more, but she didn't want to push him. So she sat in silence, wondering why Silas was so afraid to let his children live their lives.

The next day they decided to head out to the Kauffman farm for visiting Sunday.

"I heard they keep themselves to themselves," Silas said as the horse trotted along the narrow back roads, past snow-capped barns and white fields dotted with cattle. "Vernon and Arleta shut everyone out after their buggy accident, ain't so?"

"That's all changed since Sadie married Vernon," Mary said. "She's brought so much healing to that family. And you've seen how she loves to be around people. She's certain sure to have lots of visitors today, including *youngies* for Becky to meet."

Silas did not look pleased. "I thought there wouldn't be anyone else there but the Kauffmans…"

Mary turned to study Silas's expression. An uncomfortable twinge of anxiety flickered inside of her. Hadn't he ever been to a neighbor's house on visiting Sunday? "It will be *gut* that there will be new friends for your *kinner* to meet, ain't so?"

Silas cleared his throat and readjusted the reins in his hands. "*Ya*, *ya*, of course." But his expression said otherwise.

When they pulled onto the Kauffmans's property, Silas's expression was still grim. Mary's anxiety rose, but she said nothing. Now was not the time to discuss such things. The Kauffman twins and a group of youngies were already approaching the buggy, smiling and waving. "We haven't seen you since the wedding," a teenaged girl named Martha said as they neared. She wore a black headscarf draped over her *kapp* and tied beneath her chin. Her sharp, narrow nose was red with cold. “Is Becky with you?”

“Ya!” Becky pushed open the back door of the buggy and hopped off the bench seat onto the hard, frozen ground.

“*Kumme* with us,” Martha said. “We’re going to take care of the chores in the barn while the adults visit.” She lowered her voice to a whisper and winked at Becky. “But don’t worry, we’ll still have fun.”

Becky rushed off with them before Silas could stop her. “I’m going to tell her to *kumme* back,” Silas said as she slid out of the buggy and stalked around to Mary’s side to help her down from her seat.

“But why?” Mary asked as she leaned into his arms and dropped to the ground. It felt so good and natural for him to take her in his arms and look after her like that. It was what she had always wanted.

“Because they’re no *gut* for her.”

His words and the tone of his voice shut down the joy she had felt. “Silas, I don’t understand. I’ve known most of the *youngies* in Bluebird Hills all their lives. They've always been *gut kinner*, for the most part."

"For the most part." Silas shook his head. "It only takes one bad apple to spoil the barrel."

Mary raised her eyebrows. "*Vell*, it's a *gut* thing that Becky is a girl and not an apple then."

Silas did not respond. Instead, he began unhitching their horse from the buggy. The metal buckles jangled in the silent January air.

"Hi, Silas." A teenaged boy trotted up to them. He had a friendly freckled face, a ready smile and a gangly body from a recent growth spurt. "We didn't get a chance to meet at your wedding reception. I'm Noah."

Silas nodded but did not smile.

"I hope you're settling in to Bluebird Hills *oll recht*."

"Well enough," Silas said without enthusiasm.

"Hello, Noah," Mary said with a reassuring smile to counter Silas's standoffish attitude. "How's your *groossmammi* feeling?"

"Much better. That chicken noodle soup you brought over was just what she needed to get over her head cold."

"I'm so glad to hear that."

"Daed?" Ethan appeared at Silas's side and tugged on his sleeve. "It's freezing out here. Can we go inside?"

"Ya, ya." He rubbed his forehead, distracted. "Let's get you warm." But Silas made no move toward the Kauffmans's large, weather-beaten farmhouse. "I'll just get Red Rover settled in the barn."

"No need," Noah said as he reached for the horse's lead. "I'm headed that way. I'll see to him for you."

Silas frowned.

"*Danki*, Noah," Mary said quickly. "That's very thoughtful of you."

"Becky's there?" Noah's voice cracked and he cleared his throat. "With the other *youngies*, I mean. I was trying to find them."

Mary suppressed a smile. She was thrilled to see Noah Peachy show interest in Becky and it was cute that he was trying to hide it. He had always been a sweet boy.

Silas furrowed his brow. "Becky? What's Becky got to do with you?"

Noah flinched. "I was just asking… I mean, no one has seen her around since your wedding." He swallowed hard. "I was just looking for all the other *youngies* and was wondering…"

Mary stepped forward. "She'll be happy to see you, Noah. They're all out in the barn. Go on, now." She wrapped her arm in Silas's so that he didn't bolt after Noah. "Let him go," she whispered as Noah led Red Rover away, the horse's hooves thudding against the frozen ground. "You don't need to worry about Noah. See how *gut* he is with animals? It shows that he's got a *gut* heart. Red Rover has always liked him and that horse doesn't like anyone."

Silas grunted.

"Kumme," Mary said. She could not understand what had gotten into Silas. "Becky will be *oll recht* on her own for a few minutes. They're just going to tend to the livestock, then they'll *kumme* back to the house. It's too cold for them to go anywhere else."

Silas hesitated, then walked with Mary and Ethan past the *dawdi haus*, with its quaint tin roof and white trellis, to the farmhouse's wide front porch. They stomped the snow off their boots before knocking briefly and letting themselves in. The happy chatter of familiar voices met Mary along with a blast of warm air. "Hello!" Mary said loudly enough for the crowd to hear from the next room.

"Is that Mary?" A face popped out of the doorway to the living room. "It is!" Sadie hurried down the hallway and enveloped Mary in an enthusiastic hug. Then she turned her big, welcoming grin toward

Silas and Ethan. "*Kumme* in. We were just pouring the *kaffi*."

Vernon, Arleta, Gabriel, Eliza, Bishop Amos and his wife, Edna, were sitting in the living room. After a round of hugs and hellos, they all settled into casual conversation. Except for Silas. His eyes kept darting to the window as he took slow sips of his coffee. Mary knew he must be looking out for Becky, but why?

Ethan sat on the green sofa, snuggled between Mary and Silas, and quietly swung his feet, which didn't quite reach the floor.

"Do you want to go outside and play?" Vernon asked him after a while. "My *kinner* are sledding in the backyard with Simon and Priss."

Ethan stared at Vernon for a moment with big eyes, then shook his head without speaking.

"I'll bring you some hot chocolate to warm you up, then maybe you'll feel like going outside," Sadie said.

Ethan smiled and nodded.

"What do you say, Ethan?" Silas asked.

"Danki," Ethan said in a small voice.

Mary shifted closer to Ethan and put an arm around him. He had come a long way since he arrived in Bluebird Hills, but being around so many new people was too much for him today. After Ethan finished his hot chocolate, Mary took the mug, set it on the coffee table and said to him in a low voice, "Let's get you outside, *ya*? I'll walk you out there to find the other *kinner*."

Ethan hesitated, then nodded when a playful shout drifted in from outside. "Sounds like they're having fun, ain't so?" Mary stood up abruptly. "I'm going to go outside with Ethan," she announced to the room. "Be back in a minute."

Silas caught her eye and she saw the concern flicker across his features. Mary leaned into his ear and said softly, "I'll make sure he's *oll recht* before I *kumme* back inside."

Silas nodded, but his expression was still grim.

His reaction troubled Mary as she and

Ethan bundled into their winter coats, then headed outside into a cold blast of winter air. The sky had cleared into a brilliant blue and sunlight reflected across the sparkling snow. The sound of children laughing reached them and Mary nodded toward the direction of the noise. "I hear them."

Ethan looked down.

"Don't you want to sled with your new friends?"

Ethan shrugged.

Mary crouched down to his eye level. She could feel the cold snow against her knees through her black stockings. "What's the matter?"

He chewed on his lip and shrugged again.

"It's *oll recht.* You don't have to tell me if you don't want to, but I might be able to help if you do."

Ethan raised his eyes to meet hers. "Do you…do you think they like me?"

"Is that what's bothering you? You're afraid they don't like you?"

Ethan dropped his eyes and nodded.

"They like you, Ethan." Mary put a hand on his arm. "They want to play with you, certain sure."

"But how do you know?" Ethan kicked at a clump of snow with the toe of his boot.

"Because I know you and I know how much *I* like you."

Ethan's gaze shot up to hers. "You do?"

"Absolutely. You're the *sohn* I always wanted."

"I am?" His brow creased in concentration, as if he was trying to make sense of what she had just said. "Do you really mean that?"

"*Ya*. I really do mean that."

Ethan grinned and flung himself into Mary's arms. She held him tightly until he wriggled out of the hug and ran around the corner of the farmhouse to the children hauling a sled up a hill. Beside them was an empty field dusted with pristine snow.

Mary whispered a quick prayer of thanks when they shouted and waved Ethan over.

Mary had planned to go back to the warm, cozy farmhouse. But Ethan turned and motioned for her to follow him. When she saw the look of expectation on his face, she couldn't say no. Before Mary knew it, she was on a sled with him and Priss, flying down the hill and shrieking. They hit a snowbank at the bottom and toppled out in a heap. Ethan popped up with snow covering his face and hat. He sputtered, wiped his mouth and grinned. "That was fun!"

Priss pulled herself up and brushed off her knees. "Are you *oll recht*, Mary?"

"I sure am! I haven't been on a sled since I was your age and it was even more fun than I remembered."

Priss gave an adorable, chubby-cheeked smile. "Then let's go again!"

A sled with Ned, Newt and Simon crammed aboard soared past them. "Mary!" Ned shouted. "Bet you can't go as far as we can!"

"Challenge accepted!" Mary shouted back. She stumbled up from the snow, shook out the skirt of her dress and hurried up the hill.

Mary lost track of time as she raced the children down the hill again and again. Soon, it was hard to imagine that Ethan had almost been too shy to enjoy the fun. She was clambering onto the sled yet again when she heard Becky's high-pitched voice carry on the breeze. "You're not being fair, *Daed*!"

Mary's lighthearted mood evaporated as she felt a pang of guilt. If she had stayed with Silas, maybe she could have averted whatever problem he and Becky were having. *"Nee,"* Mary said out loud to make sure she listened. She would not think that way. She was not responsible for other people's actions, no matter what her emotions told her. The declaration gave her a surprising satisfaction. She would not have recognized that truth just a few weeks ago.

"What did you say?" Ethan asked as he adjusted his weight across the front of the sled.

Mary had not meant for anyone else to hear her. "I was just talking to myself. I need to check on something. Why don't you go on down without me this time."

"You sure?"

"*Ya*. Just keep having fun."

"Sure will!" Ethan said before launching himself down the hill with a whoop.

Mary hurried toward the side yard, the wet skirt of her dress slapping against her knees. She could hear Silas and Becky's raised voices before she could see them.

"But *Daed*—"

"*Nee*. No arguments, Becky."

They came into view as Mary rounded the corner of the sprawling farmhouse. Becky looked to be close to tears as she stood with arms crossed, an expression of defiance on her pale face.

"What's the matter?" Mary asked as she came toward them.

"Nothing," Silas said. "Everything's fine."

"Nee!" Becky hissed. "Nothing is fine!"

"Whatever's going on, I'm sure we can work it out," Mary said.

"Not unless you can make *Daed* see reason."

"I am being reasonable."

"Why don't you both tell me what's going on?" Mary asked.

Silas and Becky stared at each other silently instead of answering.

"Silas?" Mary asked gently. "What's the problem?"

He threw out his arm to motion toward to barn. "She wants to ride home with that Noah boy, go to a singing with him, get into all kinds of trouble…" He shook his head. "I'll not allow it."

"It's just a singing, *Daed*! There's nothing wrong with youth-group meetings. Would you rather me out getting into real trouble with the *Englisch*?"

"I'm sure you can get into enough trouble right here, with the Amish *youngies*!"

Mary stepped between them. *"Oll recht."* She put out her arms, palms toward each of them. "Let's take a minute to stop and breathe."

"I am breathing," Silas muttered. "And certain sure she is, too. You can't shout at your *daed* without a good breath."

"You know what I mean, Silas."

Silas grunted.

"I can't believe this." Becky's voice cracked as she struggled for words. "I've tried so hard to fit in here, but you won't let me be a normal *youngie*. You made me leave home and now you won't let me make any friends in Bluebird Hills. I'm all alone here!" Becky stuffed down a sob, then spun around and marched away. "That's it," she muttered to herself, but loudly enough for them to hear. "I'm going to find a way back to Ohio. I can't live like this anymore."

Mary let out a long, deep breath. Every muscle in her body felt tense. "What just happened?"

Silas just shook his head. "It's time to go. We made a mistake coming here. Becky should be at home, where I can keep an eye on her. She doesn't need these—" he motioned toward the barn, where the *youngies* were gathered "—so-called friends." Then he trudged toward the buggy before Mary could think of what to say.

Mary didn't know what was going on in Silas's head, but there was definitely something wrong. And it was up to her find out what it was.

Chapter Nine

Mary could hear Becky's muffled sobs through her bedroom door. She had fled to her room as soon as the family got home from visiting. Downstairs, Silas's heavy footsteps paced back and forth across the hardwood floor. Mary fidgeted with the hem of her apron as she debated what to do. Her little home had been her sanctuary when she was single. She may have endured loneliness, but she had never had to bear the stress of anyone else's anger under her roof. Mary laid her forehead against Becky's door and closed her eyes. The tension took her back to her father's long, stony silences and unjust outbursts, which made her feel trapped and small.

But she wasn't small anymore. She could do something about it now. Mary swallowed hard. She didn't want to interfere with Silas's parenting, but she knew the difference between right and wrong, and the way he was treating Becky wasn't right. Mary knew, deep inside, that it was wrong to witness Becky's pain without trying to help. She wished she could talk to Silas first, but he had avoided her ever since they got home from the Kauffman farm that afternoon.

Mary took a deep breath and gently knocked on the door. "Becky? It's me, Mary."

"What do you want?"

"I just want to *kumme* in for a minute."

There was a long pause. *"Oll recht."*

Mary eased open the door and gave Becky a sad smile. "Can I sit down with you?"

Becky shrugged. "I guess."

Mary walked across the small space and

lowered herself onto the foot of the narrow bed. Becky's eyes were red and her entire face was puffy. She must have been crying for hours.

"Did you *kumme* to tell me that *Daed* is right?"

That was a tricky question to answer. Mary didn't want to undermine Silas—especially when she didn't know his side of things yet—but she didn't want to go along with his decision, either. Mary considered her response for a moment. "I came to tell you that I'm sorry you're hurting. Do you want to talk about it?"

Becky threw up her hands. "What's there to talk about? *Daed* doesn't trust me. He never lets me do anything. I'm sixteen years old and he treats me like I'm six. I've never even been to a singing! I've never ridden home from a church service with a *bu* or done any of the things that other *youngies* do. Everyone else my age is in youth group having fun and I'm stuck here."

Mary nodded. "That sounds really tough."

"Ya." Becky looked down at the quilt and picked at a loose thread. "I'm missing out on the singing right now. *Daed* never lets me go anywhere. He was like that back home in Ohio, too."

"How does that make you feel?"

"Terrible. Like *Daed* thinks I'm a bad person, always looking for trouble." Becky's eyes flicked up to Mary. "Why doesn't he trust me?" A fat tear slid down her cheek and she wiped it with the back of her hand. "I'm not a bad person."

"Oh, Becky." Mary could not stop herself from pulling her stepdaughter into a hug. She felt so small and frail that Mary's heart ached. "For certain sure, you're not."

Mary expected Becky to pull away, but instead she collapsed against Mary's shoulder and began to sob. "He hates me."

"Nee," Mary whispered as she smoothed her hand over Becky's hair, where it had come loose from her *kapp.* "I promise he doesn't hate you."

"You don't know that," Becky choked out between sobs.

Mary continued to gently run her hand over Becky's hair. "I don't know the full story between the two of you, but I know enough to see your *daed* loves you. But even people who love each other can handle things the wrong way sometimes."

Becky pulled back, hiccupped and looked Mary in the face. "You think *Daed* is wrong?"

Mary's stomach tightened. This was an impossible situation. "*Vell*, like I said, I don't know the full story. But I do know you are not a bad person, looking for trouble."

Becky laid her head on Mary's chest and Mary retightened her arms around her. "Right now, I know it feels like nothing is going to be *oll recht*. Being sixteen can feel that way." Mary sighed. "Or any age can feel that way, if you think the people that you love don't see you for who you really are."

Becky's breath caught in her throat as

she choked on a sob. "You understand how I feel."

"I think I do. Not exactly, of course. But I know what it's like to feel unseen and unappreciated."

Becky was silent for a moment as Mary held her close. "You know my *mamm* left me."

Mary listened without responding. She didn't know the details about Becky's mother, but could certainly sense that the entire family felt abandoned.

"And now *Daed* doesn't think I'm *gut* enough, either."

Mary didn't know how to answer her. There was too much pain to wipe away with a few sentences. So she held Becky as tightly as she could for a long time, showing her love without words.

Later, after Mary slipped out of Becky's room, Silas was no longer pacing the living room. She knew it was too cold and dark for him to have taken a walk, so she suspected he had retreated to his workshop. Well, he could not hide from her. She couldn't let this go on any longer. Something had to be done to heal the pain and misunderstanding between him and his only daughter.

But confrontation was Mary's worst fear. Her stomach roiled as she made her way to the barn. The searing night air cut through her cloak and the darkness pressed in on her like never before. What would Silas say? Would he argue with her? Would he tell her she had no right to interfere, even though they were a family now? He had never raised his voice to her, but the thought of him being disappointed in her was worse than being yelled at. All she wanted was his love and approval.

But doing the right thing was more important, no matter how bad it felt.

The barn was dark and silent as she crept inside. The only sounds were the soft crunching of Red Rover eating a carrot and the low murmur of Silas's voice. As her eyes adjusted, she could make out Silas's silhouette leaning against the horse's stall. A single kerosene lantern hung from a nail, casting a flickering light across the rough wallboards, but leaving Silas in shadow. "That's a *gut bu*," he whispered as he patted Red Rover's neck and slipped him another carrot.

"Looking for me?" Silas asked without turning his attention from the horse.

"*Ya.* I thought I might find you in your shop, even though it's Sunday."

Silas gave a wry smile. "I'd be working if I could. It's a *gut* distraction."

"Everyone needs a place where they feel safe."

Silas grunted and gave the horse another good pat on the neck.

Mary waited for him say something about his argument with Becky. Instead, he shifted his weight from one foot to the other and sighed.

"Silas?"

"*Ya.*" His tone sounded resigned and defeated.

"What's going on between you and Becky?"

"Nothing. We're *oll recht*."

Mary braced herself. "She's crying her heart out in her room right now because she's missing out on the singing. She's too young to stay shut in at home all the time. Why won't you let her make friends here?"

Silas said nothing for a moment. He lowered his head and leaned his weight onto his elbows as they rested over the top of the stall. "It's too much to explain," he said after a moment.

Mary eased closer. "Try me."

Silas didn't move for a moment and Mary thought he was going to ignore her. But then he took a deep breath, let it out and said, "I have to protect her."

"Protect her from what, Silas? What danger is there in a youth singing?"

Silas's mouth tightened. He shook his head. "Plenty. I wish you could see that."

"Maybe if you explained, I could." Mary put a hand on his arm. "Please try. I want to understand."

He pushed away from the stall to face her. Mary dropped her hand and gazed up at him. His face was partially lost in shadow, but she could make out the pain in his eyes. The lantern light cast a warm, orange glow on the wall behind him. "Becky's *mamm* left us. She..." Silas frowned. "She got into trouble..." His frown deepened. It was clear he didn't want to say any more.

"I'm so sorry, Silas. I can only imagine how hard that must have been. But what does that have to do with Becky now?"

He gave her an incredulous look. "Everything."

"But that doesn't make sense."

"*Ya*, it does. Look, I'm not going to let Becky go to any singings or do anything else with Noah or any of the *youngies* here. That's the right thing to do. I wish you could understand."

"*Nee*, I can't because..." Mary squared her shoulders. Silas might be disappointed in her, but she was not going to go along with him just because he wanted her to. "Because I think you're wrong."

Silas shook his head sadly. Seeing the disapproval in his eyes was worse than if he had reacted in anger. All Mary wanted was for him to see that she was on his side. But sometimes being on a person's side meant going against them. She refused to repeat her mother's marriage. She would not tell her husband he was right in order to avoid conflict when she knew that he was, in fact, wrong.

Silas turned back toward Red Rover. "I'm sorry you feel that way, Mary," he said softly. "I care about you. I care about your opinion. But you have no idea what you're talking about when it comes to Becky."

Mary's throat felt thick. She didn't know if she could get any more words out, but she had to. "Have you tried talking to her? I don't mean talking *at* her, but actually listening to her? I just did and she had a lot to say. I think I understand more about her than you realize, even though I don't know the whole story."

A muscle twitched along the side of Silas's face. "I'm sorry, Mary. It's not going to help for me to talk to her. I've tried."

"You've tried talking but you haven't tried listening."

"You don't know that."

"I've seen enough to make a pretty *gut* guess."

"*Oll recht*. Fair enough."

"I know you are a kind, gentle man. Look at how you speak to Red Rover. And he is not an easy horse to get along with. He hardly likes anyone, but he likes you. You've earned his trust. Becky just needs the same gentleness and understanding."

"Red Rover doesn't talk back."

"*Nee*, but he sure knows how to bite."

"Becky isn't a horse. It's so much more complicated than that."

"For certain sure it is. I'm just saying that you are more capable of connecting with her than you realize."

Silas stared into the distance for a moment. Then he shook his head. "I've made up my mind. Becky stays home for her own *gut* unless she's with us."

Mary stared at him. She knew by the set of his jaw he was not going to budge. Her heart sank. She had seen that he had a kind and loving heart despite his distant demeaner, and yet he seemed unable to show his daughter the same kindness he showed everyone else. Mary knew she had done the right thing to confront him, but the conversation had left her feeling worse than ever.

Silas stayed in the barn for a long time after Mary left, too ashamed to face her. Only after he was sure she had gone to bed did he say good night to their horse, creep out of the barn and sneak into his own room. He hesitated as he passed Becky's door. He thought he heard a muffled sniffle, but wasn't sure. He raised his hand to knock. But anxiety flooded him and he dropped his hand. Becky wouldn't listen to him. She wouldn't understand. If he said anything, he was sure it would only make things worse.

The next morning, Silas couldn't face Mary at the breakfast table. He knew it had taken all her courage to confront him the night before. He had noticed the tremor in her hands as she tried to convince him to do the right thing. Ever since they married, he had recognized her fear of confrontation. He knew her father's harsh treatment had made it almost impossible for her to stand up for what she believed.

And yet she had.

It stuck Silas in that moment, as he watched Mary pour Ethan a glass of milk and ruffle his hair, that she was the bravest person he had ever met. This unassuming woman who could barely look others in the eye carried more courage than men who wore their bravado like a badge. She stood up to him even though she must have been terrified that he would reject her for it.

Instead, he loved her for what she had done.

He almost choked on his coffee when he realized that.

"*Daed?* Are you *oll recht*?"

No. He definitely was not alright.

"*Ya*. Just in a hurry to get to the workshop." He took a step backward, toward the door. "I'll, uh…just take this with me." He raised his mug. "Along with a biscuit. *Danki*, Mary. It looks wonderful good." He grabbed a ham-and-cheese biscuit from the serving platter, spun around and hurried from the kitchen before she could reply. But the emotions she stirred within him followed him across the front yard, past the row of bare maple trees and into the little white barn.

Silas did not expect Mary to join him in the workshop that day. Even though she had begun to work with him and seemed to enjoy it, she would be too frustrated to want to spend time with him. He was certainly frustrated with himself. Why couldn't he just open up to her?

Silas couldn't believe it when he heard the barn door creak open and a cold gust of wind blew in, shuffling the stack of papers on his desk. She had come to face him, in spite of his coldness the day before.

Mary leaned hard against the door to close it against the force of the wind. Then they were left staring at one another in silence.

"I'm sorry, Mary," he blurted out. "I shouldn't have shut you out yesterday."

"Do you want to try and talk about it today?"

The words were pushing against his throat, burning to come out. He had kept all his fears pushed down inside for so long. But if he told Mary everything, then she would know he had failed his family. He had not been able to keep Linda safe. He had watched her crumble and could not stop it. How could Mary love or trust him then?

"Nee."

Mary smiled, but he could see her disappointment. "*Vell*, that engine isn't going to oil itself. I'm going to get to work." She hung her cloak on a peg by the door, then looked back at him. "When you're ready to talk, I'm ready to listen."

"How...how's Becky doing today?" Silas clenched his jaw. He shouldn't have brought it up. But he was so worried about her, he couldn't stop himself.

"She's still heartbroken over missing the singing yesterday." Mary hesitated, then added gently, "You should ask her yourself."

The words stung, but he couldn't argue them. He had asked for this when he brought up the subject. Time to shut it down again.

"I've got to get this order finished." He turned his attention back to the length of nylon cord in his hand.

Mary said nothing more about it. Instead, she spent the morning tinkering with the diesel-powered engine. When she turned it on and sat back on her heels, it purred like a cat.

"It's never sounded so *gut*," Silas said.

A hint of pride passed over her face before she stamped it down. *"Danki."*

Silas wanted to tell her that she was wonderful and smart and talented. He wanted her to see that he appreciated her. He wanted to do the same for Becky. But the words were still stuck in his throat. They never seemed to get unstuck, no matter how much he tried. What else could he do to show them that he cared?

That evening, Silas shooed his family out the front door and into the buggy. He had already hitched up Red Rover. The horse stood pawing the ground with a hoof, his breath forming a little cloud in the chilly night air.

"No cooking tonight," he said to Mary after he helped her onto the bench seat and settled in beside her.

"*Daed!* I'm the one whose been doing most of the cooking since Mary started working with you in the shop. Haven't you noticed? I took over the kitchen!"

Silas sighed. He had said the wrong thing. Again. "I know, Becky. That's why I'm treating you to dinner tonight. You deserve a break, same as Mary. I'm sorry I didn't make that clear."

"Oh." Becky dropped back against her seat. *"Oll recht."* She turned her head to stare outside. "But I still feel like you don't notice how much I do. And I do it all without complaining."

"I thought you wanted to take over the kitchen work."

"I did, but that's not the point."

Silas swallowed his pride. "You're right. I'm sorry I haven't made you feel appreciated."

Mary's eyes shot to him and her face lit up. Seeing her approval made up for the sting of having to apologize when he had not meant to hurt anyone. Well, good thing he was giving them a treat tonight. That was a good start, even if he couldn't manage to actually communicate with them.

Ethan chattered from the back seat about Simon's amphibian collection as they trotted along Bluebird Hills's freshly plowed roads. "He told me all about it when we were at the Kauffmans's yesterday. Can we go see it sometime, *Daed*?"

"Sure. As long as I don't have to touch any of them."

Mary laughed. "Same."

"Wait, that's not fair." Becky leaned forward in her seat, toward her father. "Why does he get to go out to see his friends and I don't?"

Silas pinched the bridge of his nose and squeezed his eyes shut. They hadn't even made it to the restaurant yet and his good idea was already falling apart. He opened his eyes and let out a long breath. "Because it's different."

"How?"

"Uh, *vell*, Simon is younger."

"Then he needs more supervision, not less, ain't so?"

Silas glanced at Mary for help, but she just raised her eyebrows. He couldn't look to her to back him up on this. "Trouble gets more…complicated when you get older. *Youngies* get into worse things than *kinner*."

"*Daed*, I'm not going out drinking on my *rumspringa* or anything like that. But you act like I am. What kind of complicated trouble is there at a youth-group singing?"

"Don't forget about that trouble you got into in Millersburg."

"That was six weeks ago!"

"Six weeks may seem like a long time to someone your age, but not to me," Silas said.

"But I didn't drink anything. It was two other *youngies* in the group who'd brought the alcohol. I couldn't control what they did."

"*Nee*, but you can control who you spend time with, which is exactly my point.

If you hadn't gone out with them, you wouldn't have been caught in that situation."

Becky shook her head so hard that her *kapp* strings bounced against her cheeks. Then she dropped back in her seat with a thud and crossed her arms. "Next time I won't do the right thing. Because if I hadn't, you never would have known."

Mary looked at Silas, then back at Becky. "Would one of you mind telling me what happened?"

Silas's hands tightened around the leather reins. "Becky went out with some *youngies* who were on their *rumspringa* and they started drinking. Then they tried to drive the buggy home." Silas didn't want to think about this right now. It brought up everything he fought so hard to push down. Those emotions emerged, making his voice sound harsher than he meant. "*Youngies* don't realize it's dangerous to drink and drive, even if it's a buggy. *Englisch* police give DWI charges for that, you know. Don't you realize you could have been hurt?"

"Ya." Becky leaned forward again, her voice raised to match his. "That's why I found a phone and called our *Englisch* neighbor to give you the message to *kumme* get me."

Mary frowned. "So you didn't drink and you didn't let them drive after they'd been drinking?"

"Right! But *Daed* is still punishing me for doing the right thing. If I had kept my mouth shut, then I'd still have a life."

"Silas?" Mary's voice was gentle, but firm. "Is this true?"

"*Ach*, I wouldn't put it like that, exactly." How could he explain the unbearable panic that had overtaken him when he had heard the words *drinking and driving* from his own daughter's lips? It had been as if the past had come crashing in to destroy him and everything he had left to love.

"Then how would you put it?" Mary's voice was calm, but her eyes were serious. It seemed she was not going to back down.

"Look, that's not what matters. What matters is that Becky was in danger and it just proves that my instincts are right. She needs to stay at home, where I can make sure she's safe." His heart rate was increasing as he thought about it. "Becky, you got away safely that time, but what about the next time? What about the next group of friends? Something much worse could happen. I can't risk it. I love you too much."

Becky froze. "You love me?"

"*Ya*, of course!" Silas yelled. "I'm sorry." He calmed his tone and repeated himself. "I mean to say, *ya*, of course I love you."

Becky pursed her lips and looked away. Her bottom lip trembled. "*Vell*, I love you, too, *Daed*."

Silas couldn't remember the last time they had said those words to one another. Despite all the tension and frustration, he felt like grinning. "You do, huh?" He turned his head and gave her a playful wink.

"Okay, don't push it."

Silas smiled, then turned his attention back to the road. Knowing they loved one another was enough to get them through anything.

When they arrived at the Old Amish Kitchen restaurant, Silas guided the buggy beneath the shelter set aside for Amish horses and buggies. A few other horses stood at the hitching posts, swishing their tails as they dozed. As Silas pulled the handbrake, he studied the building beyond the parking lot full of *Englisch* cars. Its cheerful yellow walls and exposed wooden beams reminded him of an old-fashioned German village. Each window was lined with turquoise-green shutters and window boxes filled with plastic tulips. A wooden windmill with turquoise accents stood in the yard beside the building. Its big blades turned slowly in the crisp, winter breeze. Silas gave a nod of approval. "Reminds me of all the German architecture back in Holmes County, ain't so?"

"*Ya,*" Ethan said. "I hope the food's as *gut*, too."

"It's wonderful *gut,*" Mary said. She turned to Silas. "How did you know about this place?"

"Vernon told me about it when you were sledding yesterday. He said he takes his family here whenever they are having a bad day and need cheering up. It's always been Arleta's favorite restaurant."

"Mine, too." Mary's smile was as bright as a candle flame. Making her happy was making him happy. He wanted to tell her that, but now was not the time. His *kinner* were already jumping out of the buggy and heading toward the entrance. He hopped down, hurried to Mary's side and helped her out. Their eyes met and, just for a moment, it felt like the world stopped. All his worries about Becky faded away, forgotten somewhere in Mary's dark gray eyes. He spun her around as he lowered her to the ground, sending the skirt of her dress swooshing in a circle around her black stockings. She laughed out loud and kept her eyes on him as the world blurred around them. All he could think about was leaning in for a kiss.

"Hurry up, *Daed*," Ethan shouted over his shoulder. "I'm starving."

Silas set Mary down and gave a little smile. "He's always starving."

There would be no kiss. Maybe that was for the best. He shouldn't let himself get too carried away with emotion. Just because he was falling for Mary didn't mean that he was good for her. He had to remember that, no matter how hard it was to resist that beautiful smile that lit up her entire being.

Chapter Ten

The evening was so perfect that Mary thought she needed to pinch herself. It had started off a bit rocky, with Silas and Becky at odds with one another. But then they had both said they loved each other. Mary was excited at the progress they were making. Some things took time. She knew they still had a long way to go, but *Gott* was at work, for sure and certain.

And then, there had been that wonderful moment when Silas had spun her around and she had felt everything melt away but him. Her heartbeat had echoed his in that moment, she was sure of it. Maybe, just maybe, he was feeling for her what she was feeling for him. The thought kept her warm and cozy as she devoured her plate of chicken schnitzel, sauerkraut, potatoes and freshly baked brown bread.

"Can we have dessert, *Daed*?" Ethan asked after he ate the last bite of his bratwurst and set down his fork with a satisfied sigh.

"You sure can. Tonight's a night to have fun together, remember? You can have whatever you want."

"Why don't you go look at the dessert case in the bakery section," Mary said. "They have so many *gut* options to choose from."

"Excellent idea," Ethan said as he scooted out of the booth. "I like seeing them better than reading about them in the menu."

"I'm going, too," Becky said as she slid out of the booth behind him.

"Do you need to take a look?" Silas asked Mary.

"*Nee*, I know exactly what I want. Their Black Forest cake is too good not to get."

Silas slapped the dessert menu down on the table. "Then I know what I'm getting. No need to consider anything else."

Mary watched Ethan weave between the tables full of diners, then trot past a display of cuckoo clocks hanging on the wall. Even Becky was smiling. "This has been really nice, Silas. *Danki* for taking us all out. You made the *kinner* happy."

"Just the *kinner*?"

Mary felt herself blush. "Not just the *kinner*."

There was an awkward silence, punctuated by Mary's pounding heart. She wondered if Silas's heart was beating too fast as well.

"This has been *gut* for Becky, *ya*?" Silas looked down and fiddled with the corner of the menu. "She'll be happier about staying home now, right?"

"*Ya*, it's been *gut* for Becky to get out, but—" Mary cut herself off to take a sip of ice water. She didn't want to say anything to spoil the moment.

"But what?" Silas glanced up with concerned eyes, then looked back down. She caught the flicker of fear that danced across his face before he tightened his features. She wondered what he was hiding.

She bit her lip. "I'm sorry, Silas, I know this isn't what you want to hear. But as nice as this evening has been, it's not going to be enough for Becky. She needs to be with other people her own age. She needs to get out and live her life."

Silas sighed as he fidgeted with the menu. "You think I should let her go to youth group."

"*Ya*. I definitely do."

Silas frowned. His jaw clenched and released. Mary could see how much this was costing him. Finally, he said, "*Oll recht*. I'll let her go."

A relieved grin spread across Mary's face. "You're doing the right thing, Silas. *Danki*."

"I just hope you're right." He did not look nearly as happy as Mary felt.

"Right about what?" Becky asked as she and Ethan neared the table.

Mary's grin was still plastered on her face. "*Gut* timing. Your *daed* has something to tell you."

Ethan scooted into the booth before Becky. "I'm getting the apple strudel."

"Excellent choice," Mary said.

Becky slid into the booth after Ethan. "What do you have to tell me, *Daed*?" Becky cocked her head and stared at her father.

"I, uh…*vell*, Mary thinks, that is to say, I think Mary is right."

Mary gave him an encouraging nod.

Becky shot a confused glance from Silas to Mary, and then back to Silas.

Silas tossed up his hands. "You can go to the next youth-group meeting."

Becky gasped, then bounced up and down in her seat. "Do you really mean it, *Daed*?" She bounced right out of the booth, zipped around the corner of the table and threw her arms around her father. "*Danki!* You won't be sorry, I promise!"

Silas looked shocked for a moment, then his expression shifted into pure joy at the unexpected hug. By the look on his face, Mary could see just how much his daughter meant to him.

Becky did not stop talking for the rest of the evening. "There's going to be a volleyball game," she said between quick bites of German crumb cake. "And if we win, there's going to be a tournament. I'm pretty *gut* at volleyball, right, *Daed*?"

"*Ya*, for certain sure."

"I'm going to start practicing right away. Will you help me, Mary?"

Mary straightened in her seat. "You want me to practice volleyball with you?"

"I mean, if you don't mind?"

"Becky, I would absolutely love to. We can set up a net in the barn." Mary glanced at Silas. "Do you think there's enough room?"

He shrugged and smiled. "It will be tight, but we'll make it work." He thought for a moment. "I can rearrange some of the equipment. We won't be able to fit the entire length of the net, but we'll stretch it out as far as we can. It will do until it's warm enough to play outside."

Becky picked up the napkin from her lap and dropped it on her plate. "Can we get going? I want to set up the net tonight and play a round or two with Mary before bedtime."

"I haven't seen you this excited in a long time," Silas said.

"You've given me something to be excited about."

Silas nodded, a guarded smile appearing on his face. Mary just hoped he still remembered that he was doing the right thing when it came time to drop Becky off at youth group. Only time would tell.

Over the next two days, Becky practiced volleyball whenever she could take a break from her chores. Mary and Silas cheered her on as they worked. And Mary joined her whenever she could make the time.

"It's been a long time since I played," Mary said as she rubbed a sore spot on the ridge of her hand.

"You're still *gut*," Becky said.

"*Ach*, I don't know about that." Mary adjusted her dress and braced herself for another hit.

"Becky's right," Silas said. He sat behind one of his industrial sewing machines, feeding a long strip of nylon through it, the machine humming in the background.

"You won't be saying that when I accidently throw the ball your way and it lands on your head."

Silas and Becky laughed.

"*Nee,*" Silas said. "You really are *gut*, Mary. I didn't know you were so athletic."

Mary shrugged and smiled. "I guess I didn't, either."

"I think there's a lot about you that you don't realize," Silas said. He studied her for a moment before turning his attention back to his work. Mary felt a warm glow of excitement.

Silas was seeing her for who she was. It was more than she had ever dreamed. She had always hoped that one day she would find a man who would appreciate that she cooked and cleaned for him. But Silas appreciated her for just being her.

It felt too good to be true.

By midweek, Mary knew that it was time to bring up the subject of school to Silas again. He had been reluctant when she mentioned it before, but he would have to agree to it now. Ethan was smiling and talkative, completely transformed from the shy, frightened child she had met when he first arrived on her doorstep.

"Do you have a minute?" Mary asked on Wednesday evening as she handed Silas a mug.

"What's this?" Silas asked with an expectant smile.

"Hot apple cider."

"*Mmm.*" He closed his eyes and breathed in the fragrant steam. "It smells delicious."

"Can we sit down for a minute?"

A flicker of concern passed over Silas's face, but he sat down in one of the living room chairs. "Everything *oll recht*?"

"*Ya*. It's better than just *oll recht*. Everything's really *gut.*"

"That's great to hear." He gave her a serious look. "You're okay?"

"*Ya, ya*. I'm *gut.*"

"You're…happy?"

Mary knew that Silas was hinting at something more. He was asking if she was happy with *him*.

Mary swallowed and looked down. She could feel her cheeks heat up and knew she was blushing. "I'm happier than I've ever been."

Silas exhaled. He must have been holding his breath. "I'm—I'm happy, too."

Mary's eyes flicked back up to his. The genuine affection in them sent a ripple of joy through her. Snow drifted softly outside the window and the wind howled in the distance. Inside, the woodstove crackled and glowed orange through the grate, warming the small room. The house was silent, but for the first time the silence between them didn't feel awkward. Mary wished she could savor the moment, but she knew she had to speak up. "Silas?"

"Ya?"

"Are you ready to put Ethan in school yet? When I tried to talk about it last week, you cut off the conversation."

Silas's expression changed. He looked down at the mug in his hands. "I'd rather wait a while longer."

"I know you would, but I don't think that's what's best for Ethan." There she had said it. Her father or brother would have stormed out of the room if she had dared to contradict them or push the truth on them. But Silas sat in silence. He suddenly looked very tired as he gripped the mug between his fingers and stared into the cider. "I don't know..."

"Don't you think he should go to school?"

"*Ya*, but..." His eyes stayed down. "What if he's not ready? What if he falls in with *kinner* who are bad for him and they lead him astray?"

Mary's brow crinkled. "But he's just a boy. What do you think could happen?"

"*Ach*, I don't know." Silas shifted in his seat. "He could meet friends who tempt him away from the faith."

"It's definitely wise to be careful who we spend time with so that we don't fall into worldly ways, but I think you're being overly cautious. He's too young to worry about that yet. Right now, he just wants to play outside and have fun."

"Unlike Becky, who's a step away from disaster."

Mary flinched. "I wouldn't say that. Sure, the risk of leaving the faith is greatest at her age, but she's got a *gut* head on her shoulders. And she really wants to please you."

Silas grunted.

"We could take Ethan tomorrow. He already has friends who go to the Amish school here. They played together really well at the Kauffmans's house last visiting Sunday. I think Ethan will adjust easily. He's going to like being there with them."

"I don't suppose I have a choice."

"*Nee*. I believe Bishop Amos is going to say something sooner or later if we don't put Ethan in school."

Silas didn't respond for a moment. The room felt very quiet and still as the snow drifted down beyond the windows. "It hasn't been easy, you know."

Mary sensed that Silas was trying to tell her much more than he was saying. "I know."

Silas's face tightened. "Will, uh…will you go with us?"

"I certain sure will."

Silas was surprised how easy it was to leave Ethan at the schoolhouse the next morning. He had expected to feel that deep, stomach-churning anxiety that had plagued him since Linda left them. But when Mary turned to him with her calm, reassuring smile, he felt like everything would be okay. He still scanned the schoolyard for any potential threats, but overall, he felt an unexpected peace.

Ethan had clung to his and Mary's side for only a few minutes, watching the clusters of children bundled in their black winter outerwear playing in the snow. Then he scampered away to join a group of boys making snowballs behind the water pump. His excited grin said it all.

"Let's go," Mary said in a quiet voice as she slid her arm in his. "It will be easier if we leave quickly."

"*Ya*. He looks happy. I think he's going to be *oll recht*."

Mary squeezed his arm. "I know he is."

Now, if Silas could just get through this Sunday, when Becky would go to youth group alone. There would be plenty of adults chaperoning the event, but that didn't mean bad apples couldn't slip through their supervision. Worries over Becky's safety had always weighed him down like an iron ball lodged in his belly. No matter what he did or how much he tried to distract himself, that weight was always there in the background, reminding him that his daughter was in potential danger.

Silas could not stop Sunday from coming. And when it did, Becky's joy almost made him feel good about letting her go to youth group. Almost. He still found himself eyeing the young men in the congregation as they sang the traditional German hymns from the *Ausbund* during the morning's service. Afterward, during the midday meal, he paid attention to what the teenaged girls were chatting about as they served the menfolk their food and black coffee. Silas didn't catch anything suspicious, but any one of those *youngies* could potentially lead Becky astray. Wicked intentions were not always easy to spot.

"You don't need to look so grim," Mary whispered as she swept by with a tray full of coffee mugs balanced in her hands. "I know what you're thinking and I'm certain sure it will be *oll recht*."

Silas couldn't help but feel lighter and more cheerful anytime Mary spoke to him. Maybe she was right and he just needed a reminder that the world wasn't as dangerous as he assumed it was.

Silas blew across the top of his mug of black coffee as he watched the teenagers mingling and laughing with one another. His eyes shifted to where Mary stood beside one of the makeshift tables in the Yoders's living room, collecting empty mugs and setting them on her tray. She had shown him that there was a future and a hope for him and his family, just like the scriptures said.

It was time to start believing that.

Even so, by that evening, he had almost lost his nerve. But with a gentle nod from Mary, he was able to take a deep breath, exhale and watch Becky scamper out of the buggy, into the Millers's yard.

"Remember, I've known the Millers for years," Mary said as they watched Becky tramp through the snow on her way to the massive red barn. "And Gabriel is my nephew. Plus, Eliza is the biggest stickler for the rules that I've ever known. They'll all keep a *gut* watch over Becky tonight."

"Sure. Let's go before I change my mind." Silas's instincts warned him to run after Becky, order her back into the buggy and drive her safely back home. Instead, he slapped the reins and clicked his tongue. "Walk on, Red Rover."

That night, Gabriel and Eliza dropped Becky off on their way home. She burst through the door with ruddy cheeks and sparkling eyes. "You'll never believe it!" she shouted.

"What?" Mary rushed into the living room, a damp dishrag in her hands.

"What's happened? Is everything *oll recht*?" Silas jumped up from his chair, the copy of *The Budget* newspaper in his lap falling to the floor.

"It's better than *oll recht*!" Becky clasped her hands together and did a little jump of excitement. "I won the volleyball game for my team. Can you believe it? I scored more points than anybody else."

"Well done," Silas said. He felt her contagious excitement. Maybe he could get used to Becky getting out more.

"Wow! That's *wunderbar*!" Mary dashed over and threw her arms around Becky.

"And listen, that's not all of it." Becky's grin widened as she stepped back from the hug to catch Silas's eye. "You'll never guess! Because we won this game, our youth group gets to go to the tournament in Pinecraft two weeks from now! And they want me to go with them! They said we'll win certain sure if I'm on the team."

Silas froze. He knew everything had been too good to be true. A trip to Florida with a bunch of rowdy *youngies* on their *rumspringa*? This was going too far.

"You know you can't go to Florida." His tone made it clear that this was not up for discussion.

The room went silent, as if all the joy had been sucked out of it. Both Mary and Becky turned their heads toward him, their grins replaced with expressions of disappointment.

Becky's mouth opened and closed, but no words came out. She shook her head. "You can't be serious," she finally managed.

"Pinecraft is full of trouble. Haven't you heard about all the *youngies* who gather at the public park, drinking late into the night? I've heard police have had to get involved."

"But that doesn't have anything to do with me!" Becky glanced at Mary with pleading eyes, then looked back at her father. "I'm going to play volleyball, not to get into that kind of trouble."

"*Nee*, you're not going. Not to play volleyball. Not for any reason."

"How can you do this to me?"

"You'll thank me later. I'm doing this for your own *gut*." Silas softened his voice. He had to make her see. "Please, Becky. Try to understand."

"I understand perfectly well. You don't trust me. You've never trusted me."

Silas ran a hand through his hair. He didn't know how to explain. Where would he start? There was a decade of pain and fear to unravel.

When he didn't speak, Becky shook her head again. "I'm not staying here and living like this, *Daed*. If you won't let me have a normal life, then I'm going back to Holmes County. I can stay with the Lantz cousins."

"Becky, be reasonable."

"I *am* the one being reasonable, *Daed*." Then she ran out of the room and fled up the stairs.

Silas felt like the wind had been knocked out of him. He let out a long, deep breath and sat down hard in his chair. He could feel Mary's eyes on him from across the room. He could not look up at his wife or meet her eyes. And he certainly couldn't explain to her why things had to be this way.

Mary stood in silence for a moment before she quietly set the dishrag down on the end table and sat beside him. "You seem pretty afraid that something will happen to Becky. Do you want to talk about it?"

"Nee."

Mary clasped her hands together and waited. She was able to sit so still and calm that it unnerved Silas. He could see that she had a lifetime of practice dealing with difficult people.

Was he becoming one of those difficult people now?

The thought sent a stab of remorse through him. He couldn't deal with any of this. "There's nothing to talk about," he barked at her, standing up quickly. "I'm going to bed."

Mary leaped up from her seat. “Silas, wait. You can’t make this go away by hiding from it.”

“I’m not hiding. I’ve made my decision. It’s the right one. And that’s all there is to it. Becky doesn’t know what’s best for her. She’ll get over it.” Even as Silas said the words, they felt all wrong.

“Silas.”

Something in Mary’s tone caught Silas’s attention. He had never heard her speak to him that way. Her voice sounded so sad and distant that it made his throat ache. “You remind me of my *daed* and *bruder* right now. They would make unilateral decisions, no matter what anyone else felt about it. Even if it hurt the other person. No discussion. They made the rules. Period.”

“You can’t think I’m like them…”

“*Nee*. I don’t. Because I can tell you are driven by concern for your *dochder*. I think you truly want what’s best for her, not just what’s best for you. My *daed* and *bruder* only ever cared about themselves. But something is driving you to control Becky far too much. And if you don't do something about it, you're going to make your own fears come true. You're going to drive her away."

"At least then I'll know I did everything I could to protect her."

"Silas, you have to see that isn't logical."

Silas knew Mary was right. But the fear and anger were bubbling up from deep within and surging through him. The injustice of it all was blinding him. "Please don't tell me how to think." He managed to say the words gently. But by the look in Mary's eyes, he had still made himself clear. "You can't possibly know what I think…what I've been through, why I have to keep Becky safe."

"*Nee*, I can't, especially when you shut me out. But I do know a hurt *maedel* when I see one."

"I'm keeping her from far worse hurts. If the two of you can't see that, then there's nothing I can do or say to convince you otherwise." Why couldn't Mary see that he was doing what he had to do and that it was breaking him to disappoint Becky? He would do anything for his daughter. Anything. Even if it meant that she never forgave him.

Mary stared into his eyes, unflinching. She did not understand. Maybe because she had never been through what he had.

Or maybe, because he was wrong.

Silas pushed away the thought, turned from Mary's stony gaze and left the room without saying another word.

Chapter Eleven

Word traveled fast through the Amish telegraph. Without cell phones or television to occupy them, most Plain folks in Bluebird Hills spent their time noticing their neighbors. Mary said nothing about Silas's decision, but Becky must have mentioned it when they went grocery shopping, because Viola Esch showed up on their doorstep soon after the outing.

Mary never thought she would be relieved to see the elderly busybody. But the situation with Silas felt like a lump in her throat that wouldn't go away. She could barely get food down. Mary knew that Silas was nothing like her father or brother. But his attitude was triggering the same emotions that theirs always had. She had seen that Silas was a reasonable, thoughtful man. Yet, he was not being reasonable about Becky. On the surface, it seemed like he didn't care about her feelings or needs at all.

"*Vell*, I've heard everything," Viola announced as she handed Mary her cloak and bonnet, then hobbled over to the upholstered armchair.

"Everything?" Mary asked.

"Enough, anyway." Viola waved her hand in a vague, circular motion. "You'll fill me in on the rest." She leaned her weight on the cane and eased into the chair. "Ahh. Now that feels *gut* on my old bones. Nothing like a nice sit-down in the afternoon. I'll take a cup of that blackberry tea you make."

"Oll recht."

"And I'll also take some of those snickerdoodles that you bake," Viola called after Mary as she headed for the kitchen. "Pie, if you don't have any cookies."

"You're in luck. I do have snickerdoodles."

"That's my girl."

Five minutes later, Viola and Mary were nibbling cookies beside the woodstove, one of Mary's handmade quilts draped over Viola's knobby knees. "So," she said between bites. "I hear Silas won't let Becky go to the volleyball tournament with the other *youngies*."

"Nee."

"Why not?"

"*Ach*, you'd have to ask him."

"Oh, I intend to. I stopped by his workshop on my way inside." Viola glanced at the clock on the wall. "He should be in any minute now." The doorknob turned and Viola nodded. "Right on time." Silas might be new to their community, but he had already caught on that nobody in Bluebird Hills dared to say no to Viola Esch. She gave a satisfied nod as Silas stepped inside with a gust of cold air. "I was just telling Mary that you'd be here."

"Would you have left me alone if I didn't show up?"

"Of course not. Now sit down and let's all talk about this."

Silas sighed as he lowered himself into a chair.

"Why isn't Becky going to the volleyball tournament?"

"No small talk first?" Silas asked.

"What's the point of that? We all know what I'm here for."

"Right." Silas rubbed his temples. "Go ahead."

"*Nee*, you go ahead. I'm the one who asked you a question."

"I don't have anything to say."

"Hogwash. You could start by explaining why you're keeping her home."

"This is my family and my house. What I say goes. That's all the explanation I need to give."

Mary inhaled sharply. Silas sounded a lot like her father.

Viola's eyes narrowed like she was ready to do battle. "Do you really mean that, young man?"

Silas snorted. "I haven't been 'young manned' in a long time."

"I'm your elder, ain't so? I've got decades of wisdom on you, like it or not."

Silas began to rub his temples again.

"Now, stay on subject," Viola said. "Did you mean what you said?"

Mary's chest tightened when Silas didn't answer. "You don't care what we think or feel?" she asked in a surprisingly strong voice.

"Now that's a bit much." Silas looked away. His jaw flexed.

"Is it?" Viola asked. "If the shoe fits, wear it."

Seconds ticked by. The only sound was the second hand of the clock and the distant clip-clop of horse hooves on the road beyond the frost-coated windows. Silas kept his stony expression as Mary and Viola stared at him. He glanced over at Mary, then looked away. "Of course, I care about how you feel. I shouldn't have said what I did. This is your house and your family as much as mine. I'm sorry."

"Gut." Viola nodded. "Glad we got that straight. Now, tell us what's wrong. Why are you so against Becky being a part of the youth group?"

"I let her go to youth group. But that's a lot different than letting her traipse down to Florida with a bunch of strangers."

"Edna and I are going as chaperones," Viola said. "Do you really think those *youngies* are going to get away with anything on our watch?"

Silas didn't answer.

"And we're certain sure not strangers. No one in Bluebird Hills is. Except for you. And haven't we all welcomed you with open arms?"

"Ya."

"But we've hardly seen Becky. Why are you keeping her shut away?"

"I told you, I let her go to youth group."

"That's a start, but one outing is hardly enough. She needs to be part of the community now."

"I'm doing the best I can."

Mary could see the conflict in Silas's eyes. "But why is it so wrong for Becky to be a part of things?"

"It isn't wrong…it's just…" His gaze slid over to Viola. "Nothing. Never mind. I can't explain it."

"Please try," Mary said.

"Becky just needs to trust me."

"Trust goes both ways, Silas." Mary's brow creased with emotion. "Can't you see that she can't trust you when you don't trust her? You're driving her away. It hurts so much to watch it happen and not be able to do anything to stop it."

"I see a lot, Mary." His voice sounded sad and resigned.

Mary exhaled. "I don't want to interfere with your parenting or come between you and your *dochder*. I feel like I'm in an impossible situation, caught between you both." Mary snapped her mouth closed. She couldn't believe she had said so much in front of Viola. She should have known better. But everything had just come pouring out.

"*Vell*, I've done my job." Viola pushed herself up with her cane.

"What?" Mary looked at her with confusion.

"I got you to say what you needed to say to him. I know you, Mary. Mousy Mary, they used to call you because you were so timid and quiet. You couldn't stand up to a flea. So I came here to make sure you got out what you needed to say to your husband."

Mary shook her head. "Was this some kind of…marriage counseling?"

Viola cackled. "I ought to charge for it. Now, wrap me up a few of those snickerdoodles to go, why don't you? I'll take that as payment for services rendered."

A few minutes later Viola was hobbling to the front door with a cookie tin tucked beneath one arm. "She's really something," Silas muttered as soon as the door shut behind her.

"*Ya*, but that's what's great about her, ain't so?"

Silas raised an eyebrow. "Great at meddling, you mean."

Mary wanted to enjoy a moment of humor with Silas, but she suddenly felt exposed after all she had divulged while Viola was there. "I've got to get supper on."

"Wait," Silas asked. "Did you mean what you said?"

Mary took a deep, steadying breath. She refused to ever be Mousy Mary again. *"Ya,"* she said with quiet confidence. "I did."

Silas's face hardened. "You can't understand, Mary."

"How can I when you won't give me a chance? You won't stop shutting me out."

"This doesn't concern you."

"You know that it does. We're all in this together, now."

Silas looked like he might say something, but then he tightened his mouth and shook his head. "Some things I have to handle on my own. It's for the best."

"Letting Becky have a life here is what's for the best."

"I'm her father. I know what's best for her."

"I didn't mean to imply that you didn't… But Silas, I have an outside perspective on this. I can see what you can't."

Silas stared at nothing for a moment. Mary could see the fatigue on his face. He rubbed his eyes and sighed. "I can't let her go." He stood up without looking at her. "I'm going back to work."

"But…" Mary held up her hands. "We have to resolve this."

"It is resolved. Becky stays here. End of discussion."

"Can't we talk about it, at least? So we can try to understand each other?"

"I'm sorry, Mary. I've made up my mind." Silas then stalked out of the house, into the cold winter air.

Silas stayed in his workshop as much as he could for the next few days. He couldn't face Mary after shutting down their communication. He thought about her perspective as he oiled a leather harness. He was doing himself a disservice not to consider her advice. Wasn't the point of marriage to have someone to help you navigate the difficulties of life? Why was he forcing himself to go it alone when he didn't have to?

Because he had too much to lose, that's why.

He had spent years rebuilding his image, trying to prove that he was capable and good, despite having failed his first wife. Now, he had finally found someone to love and trust again. He couldn't risk losing her. If she knew his failures and vulnerabilities… Silas shook his head as he rubbed the rag along the long strip of leather, the metal buckles jangling as he worked. The finished harness looked good and he knew the Yoders would be satisfied with it. If only he could control his life as easily as he could control the work of his hands.

Becky had continued to practice volleyball, despite Silas's refusal to let her go to the tournament. He tried to ignore her as she hit the ball on the other side of the barn, her brow creased with determination. It made his heart ache to watch, so he kept his head down, eyes on his sewing machine, as the needle punched in and out of a strip of leather. When he glanced up again, Mary was playing against Becky, her expression strained. When she saw him watching, the look of disappointment on her face nearly broke him. He wanted her to agree with him. That would make life so much easier.

But he didn't want her to agree with him just for the sake of agreeing. If he was wrong, he wanted her to stand up for what was right and encourage him to see the truth. Well, in theory, anyway. In practice, it was hard to know she disagreed with him. When he stopped to ask himself why it bothered him so much, Silas realized with a slow, sinking feeling that it was because he doubted his own decision. Mary's dissent made him uncomfortable because somewhere, deep down, he suspected she was right.

That was too much to deal with so he pushed the thought away. He had to protect Becky. Period.

After the volleyball game ended and Mary left to get Ethan from school, Becky picked up a plastic bucket full of soapy water and a scrub brush. Silas tried to ignore her as she scoured the baseboards and the scent of pine-scented cleaner filled the room. Ever since Silas had banned her from the tournament, Becky had become fastidious with her cleaning, spending her free time scrubbing every surface of the harness shop until it shined. He hadn't asked her to do all the extra work and it made him feel vaguely guilty.

The barn door swung open and Ethan came trotting inside. "Hi, *Daed*! I've just had my after-school snack and I'm ready to help you."

Mary followed behind Ethan, looking pleased at his progress.

Silas set down his rag and smiled. "How was school today?"

"It was fun. We had a snowball fight during recess. And the teacher said my cursive is looking really *gut*."

"I used to always get the capital *T* and *F* mixed up when I was learning cursive," Silas said.

"Me, too, but not anymore."

"That's really *gut*, *sohn*. It sounds like you're adjusting to your new school, *ya*?"

"*Ya*. I like it. Especially since I get to see Simon every day. Sometimes he even brings his pets to school. Yesterday he hid a salamander in his lunch pail and carried his sandwich inside his coat. The sandwich got kind of squished, but he said it was worth it."

"Sounds like you're having fun with your new friends."

Ethan nodded as Becky's scrub brush swooshed in the background. Silas shot her an uncomfortable glance. She was frowning, but did not say anything. Silas knew it wasn't fair that he encouraged Ethan to have friends, while keeping them from Becky. But Ethan didn't face the same risks that Becky did—and it had still taken all of Silas's willpower to allow his son to start at a new school, full of strangers.

The afternoon passed slowly as Ethan and Mary worked in the shop alongside Silas while Becky swept, dusted, scrubbed and polished in the background. As the sun neared the horizon and shadows overtook the interior of the barn, Becky straightened up and stretched her back. "I'll go see to supper."

Mary looked up from her worktable. "I can help."

"No need. I've got it. You can finish your work here."

"*Danki*, Becky. You're such a big help."

Becky didn't say anything in response, but she had a look of satisfaction on her face.

As soon as Becky left, Mary set down the awl in her hand and looked over at Silas. "Do you know why she's been working so hard?"

Silas shrugged. He had his suspicions, but didn't want to think about it.

Mary's gaze shifted to Ethan. "I noticed the woodpile in the living room is getting low. Would you please go fetch some wood and stack it beside the woodstove? Then we can keep the house toasty warm when we go in for supper."

"Sure," Ethan said before skipping outside. A long ray of evening sun shone into the barn when he opened the door, highlighting the dust motes in the air. Then the door creaked shut again, cutting off the light.

Mary stood up, found the book of matches and lit the clunky propane lamp beside the worktables. Orange light flickered and spread across the room, casting a warm glow across her face. Silas stopped and stared, taken in by her simple beauty. He hadn't thought her beautiful when they'd first met. But now that he knew her, everything about her had become beautiful.

"Silas, I want to talk about why Becky has been working so hard."

Silas sighed. He had known this was coming. "*Oll recht*. But I wish we could talk about something else. This is all we ever talk about. I want there to be more to our relationship than the problems with my *kinner*."

"I do, too. But we have to keep talking about it because you're not doing anything to solve the problem. And as long as the problem is there, we have to deal with it."

Silas gave a wry half smile. "Are you trying to tell me that stuff doesn't go away just because you ignore it?"

Mary smiled. "You're catching on."

Silas's face dropped back to a serious expression. "Go ahead. Let's get this over with."

"*Nee*, this isn't something to rush through. You need to face it. *Really* face it."

Silas could see the pulse in Mary's neck and the tightness in her face. She was nervous, but working hard to hide it. He didn't want her to be stressed to talk to him. He took a deep breath and tried to soften his expression. "Go ahead, Mary. I'm listening."

"Becky is working so hard because she wants to impress you."

"*Ya*. I see that. She's trying to butter me up and get on my *gut* side so I'll give her what she wants."

"*Vell*, *ya*, that's some of it. But it's much more than that."

Silas frowned and set down the rag in his hand. "What do you mean?"

Mary paused as she gathered her thoughts. She was always so careful with her words. He admired that about her. Too many people spoke before they thought. "She's trying to earn your love and approval, Silas. She's trying to be *gut* enough for you."

Silas shifted uncomfortably in his seat.

Mary looked down. "I know what that's like. It eats away at you slowly, every day, until you lose yourself in it."

Silas felt a rush of remorse. "Mary… I…"

"I know, Silas. You love Becky and you want what's best for her. I can see that. But *gut* intentions can still hurt people."

"You really think I'm hurting her? I'm just trying to protect her."

"You're making her feel like she has to prove herself to you. She knows you don't trust her. She thinks that you think she's bad—and how could she not? You show her over and over again that she's not worthy of trust, that it's an inevitable fact that she's going to go astray."

"*Nee*..." Silas swallowed hard. "I'm just trying to prevent that."

"But why do you think she needs protecting? I know bad things can happen in life, and that's always scary for parents. But this goes far beyond normal fears. You must see that."

Silas studied the woodgrain on the worktable. This was his chance to tell Mary the truth. But once he did, he could never go back again. She would know his darkest secret. Silas's eyes flicked up to Mary's calm and steady expression. If she could face him with that quiet strength of hers, then he could somehow find the courage to face her.

"It's Becky's mother."

"Oh." Mary's brow creased as she focused on Silas's words.

Silas let out a long, slow breath. "She was always troubled, even before we married. I thought things would be different after we said our vows and had our first child. But she just got worse. It was like she had a hole inside her heart that nothing could fill. And, instead of turning to *Gott*, she turned away from the faith to try to fill it. She was reckless, angry. She started drinking. And then, one day, when Ethan was just a *boppli*, she left and never came back. We didn't hear from her for months. Until an *Englisch* police officer showed up at our house to tell us the terrible news. Linda had learned how to drive when she left the Amish, but she hadn't stopped drinking. That caused an accident and she lost her life."

The shame swept through him in a hot wave. "So, as you see, I failed her and she died. I cannot fail Becky. I *will* not fail Becky."

Mary stood up from her worktable and stepped toward him. Her expression was full of compassion. There was no condemnation. But that only made him feel worse. He didn't deserve her understanding.

"Silas, I don't know what to say." She put a warm hand on his shoulder. "Except that it's not your fault. And that I am so, so sorry that happened to you and your *kinner*. A loss like that..." Mary sighed. "*Vell*, you just don't get over it."

"*Nee*, you don't."

"But, with *Gott*'s help, you find a new path, through the pain." Her hand tightened on his shoulder. "The best thing you can do is live your best life from now on. Make the most of what God has given you. Take His redemption. Don't waste it."

"But, Mary, can't you see that I failed Linda? If I had been a better husband..." Silas dropped his head into his hands. "Somehow..."

"Nee!" The force of Mary's voice snapped his head back up. "This isn't about you. You can't control anyone else's choices. You aren't responsible for their actions." She stopped and steadied her voice. "I should know, Silas. I've spent my whole life trying to be *gut* enough for my *daed* and *bruder*.

I tried so hard to make them love me, to convince them to treat me with respect. But no matter what I did, it wasn't enough for them. They took and took, until they nearly sucked the life right out of me. Mousy Mary, that's what they turned me into." She took a steadying breath and raised her chin. "But not anymore, Silas. I finally realize my worth. It's time you realized yours, too."

Silas sat in silence, considering her words.

"You're making Becky feel like she has to be *gut* enough for you. You're not doing it with the same bad intentions as my *daed* and *bruder*, but the outcome will be the same, nonetheless." Mary shook her head. "It's a terrible thing waiting to happen. You're trying to help Becky, but instead you're making her feel unseen and unappreciated. She will find someone who will give her the approval she wants…even if they're bad for her. You could push her into running off to find her freedom or into a bad marriage that hurts her, just like you went through. Patterns repeat for a reason, Silas."

The truth of Mary's words hit Silas like a punch in the gut. "Do you think it's too late?"

"It's never too late with *Gott*. He's full of second chances."

Silas let that concept wash over him. He closed his eyes and exhaled. *"Oll recht."* He opened his eyes. "But I don't know where to start. I'm so afraid that Becky will make the same choices her *mamm* did."

"Becky is her own person. She's not her *mamm*. Didn't you say that Linda was already deeply troubled by the time she was Becky's age?"

"Ya."

"Despite everything she's been through, Becky has been remarkably resilient. She hasn't shown any signs of going down Linda's path."

"Blood is strong…"

"But it isn't set in stone. We all make our own way."

Silas slowly nodded his head. "You're right, Mary." He kept nodding thoughtfully. "You're right." But Silas still felt uneasy. He tugged at his collar. It was too tight around his throat. "Mary?"

"*Ya?*"

"You really don't think it's my fault that my wife ran off? That I couldn't protect her from herself?"

"*Nee.* No more than you think I'm a failure. I couldn't stop my *daed* or *bruder* from going their own way."

"You? A failure? Never." Silas shook his head. He realized he was smiling. "That's *lecherich.*"

"No more ridiculous than you thinking you're a failure."

"You know what?" His smile widened into a grin. He could not remember ever feeling this free. It was as though an iron yoke had lifted from his shoulders.

Mary's smile widened to match his. "What?"

"We make a pretty *gut* team."

Mary stared into his eyes. As he felt the

intensity of her gaze, the mood shifted. He stood up from his chair.

"Ya," Mary whispered. "We do."

But Silas barely heard her words. He was too busy falling into those dark gray eyes. She had shown him who he really was. She had seen him and reached him when no one else had. He had never felt a connection like this with anyone else. His hand reached out to touch her face. He gently slid the back of his knuckles along the plane of her cheek. Her skin felt so soft and warm. She blushed beneath his fingers, but she didn't break eye contact.

"Can I kiss you, Mary?"

She stared into his eyes. The room was so still and silent he could hear his pulse in his ears. He had never felt so alive, so fulfilled. *"Ya,"* she answered softly.

Silas leaned down to her just as the barn door crashed open. They both jumped back as if they'd touched a hot stove. Ethan stepped inside, rubbing his hands together and shivering. "I finished bringing in the wood. It's sure cold out there."

Before they responded, Mary and Silas exchanged a quick, conspiratorial glance. Mary's blush deepened and she dropped her eyes. But she was smiling.

"*Danki*, *sohn*. Now, let's get back to work." As Silas picked up a square of leather, he knew that work would never be the same again. Nothing in life would never be the same again. Not since Mary had come into his life and changed everything with her love.

A love that he now knew they shared.

Chapter Twelve

Everything made sense now. Mary understood why Silas had put up walls and fought so hard to protect Becky, even when it harmed more than helped.

And Mary knew that he understood her, too. She had revealed her deepest hurts and failures and he had responded by revealing his own secret. And then, he had asked to kiss her.

It had been the most wonderful moment of her life.

Of course, one of the children had interrupted. That was married life. One day they might even laugh about it together.

Somehow, against all odds, she had married a stranger who understood her and, maybe, even loved her.

Love. Could it be true? Silas had all but said the words. The excitement was a roaring fire inside her belly. She could not stop smiling.

The next morning, Silas pulled Mary aside. A look of determination passed over his face. "I've decided I'm going to let Becky go to Pinecraft."

Mary grinned. "You are?"

"Ya." He gave her a sheepish smile. "I got some *gut* advice that it's the right thing to do."

"*Danki* for listening," Mary said. She had never felt so seen or heard. She wanted to lean into his arms, right then and there, but there were eggs to fry and biscuits to pull from the oven before they burned. And Ethan couldn't find his clean socks to wear to the church service. Mary glanced at the wall clock. "*Ach,* we're going to be late."

Becky's footsteps pounded down the stairs. She shot into the living room and rushed to the living-room window with her shoes clutched in her hand. The sound of hoofbeats on pavement thumped in the distance. "*Daed*, my friend Martha is driving past. She said I could ride with her to church this morning. Can I? Please? We'll go straight there."

Silas looked conflicted for a moment, but he took a deep breath, forced a smile and said, "*Ya*, go on. And you can go back to youth group tonight, too."

Becky spun around from the window. "Really? You mean it?"

"I said *ya*, didn't I?"

"Danki!" Becky grabbed her shoes and stuffed her foot into one while still walking. She hopped a step and then shoved her foot into the other one. "Bye, *Daed*! Bye, Mary!"

Mary chuckled as the door slammed shut behind Becky. "She wasn't going to give you time to change your mind."

Silas chuckled. "For certain sure."

"It might be hard at first, but you'll get used to her going out."

Silas nodded. *"Ya."* He rubbed the back of his neck. "But you're right. It's not feeling very *gut* right now."

Mary checked the clock again. "*Vell*, you won't have time to worry about it this morning. We've got to run before we're late for the service."

The rest of the day unfolded quickly. They stayed longer than usual after the service, chatting with Gabriel and Eliza, who ended up coming over to their house for supper that evening. As Eliza, Mary and Becky worked to throw together a simple Sabbath meal, Silas and Gabriel relaxed by the woodstove in the living room, discussing the latest news from that week's issue of *The Budget* newspaper.

So, when it came time for Becky to leave for youth group, Silas had not had a chance to sit down with her and talk about going to Pinecraft. Mary knew that Silas wanted to lay out some ground rules when he told her that she could go. It wasn't a conversation to have as she was running out the door, or while they were entertaining company.

Gabriel and Eliza offered to drop off Becky on their way home and she climbed into the back of their buggy with the widest grin Mary had ever seen on her. She was a different person from the sad, surly teenager Mary had met a few weeks ago.

"How about a game of Dutch Blitz?" Mary asked after they watched the buggy rumble away.

"Ya!" Ethan ran to fetch the box of cards from the hall closet.

"It'll be a *gut* distraction," Mary whispered to Silas as soon as Ethan was out of earshot. "I know you're worried about Becky."

"I am, but I'm trying my best not to be."

"I'd say you're doing a pretty *gut* job of letting go."

Silas raised his eyebrows. "It doesn't feel like it."

Mary laughed. “You’ll get used to it. Just give it time. And in the meantime, you deserve to relax and have a little fun. But I have to warn you, I never lose at Dutch Blitz.”

“Is that a challenge?”

“You bet it is.”

They played rounds of cards by the light of the propane lantern, near the warmth of the woodstove. Outside, the wind howled through the bare branches of the maple trees, but inside, wrapped beneath a quilt and leaning against Silas’s shoulder, Mary had never felt so cozy and snug.

It wasn’t until they hugged Ethan good-night and sent him up to bed that Silas began to pace the small room. He could only go four steps on his long legs before having to spin around and head in the opposite direction.

“She’ll get home safely,” Mary said in a gentle voice.

“I know. But it doesn’t feel like it.”

Mary reached out as he strode past and grabbed his hand. Silas jerked to a stop and gazed down at their hands with a look of surprise on his face. The expression quickly shifted into a smile. Mary felt a ripple of excitement. She had dared to take his hand and he was happy that she had.

"I promise, it will be *oll recht,*" Mary said as she kept her hand firmly around his. "Becky may not always do exactly what you want, but she'll stay in the faith. She wants so badly to do the right thing."

"You really think so?"

"*Ya*. It's clear as day to me."

The clip-clop of hooves hitting pavement echoed in the distance.

"That must be her," Silas said and squeezed Mary's hand. The hoofbeats grew louder and an open buggy appeared on the street, highlighted beneath the shine of the streetlight. Inside, Becky sat on the front bench seat, bundled beneath a blanket, laughing and gazing up at the man driving. The bass from a stereo system thudded through the night air. Silas's expression tightened with every beat.

He broke free from Mary's hand and stormed toward the window. "She's not with Martha."

Mary stood up.

"It's that boy Noah. He's brought her home in a courting buggy." Silas turned around and Mary saw the fear and anger on his face. "He's trying to court my *dochder*. I haven't given them permission for that." He shook his head. "Becky's too young."

"She's sixteen, Silas," Mary said gently. "That's the age when *youngies* court in Bluebird Hills."

"Not my *youngie*."

"But it's expected for her to ride home with a *bu*. And it's an open buggy. It's the proper way to do things."

Silas's jaw clenched and released, clenched and released. He shook his head. "*Nee*. I can't allow this. Noah's on his *rumspringa*. He's got to be drinking and maybe worse… He's even got a stereo installed in his buggy like an *Eng-*

lischer. That's proof enough that he's up to no *gut*."

"Lots of *buwe* put stereos in their courting buggies on their *rumspringa*. It's harmless."

Silas snorted. "It's still a bad sign. Listening to worldly music on a stereo. What's next?" He shook his head again. "*Nee*, too much could go wrong. Riding to church with Martha and going to a chaperoned youth group is one thing. Riding home with Noah—getting courted by Noah—is too much. I knew something like this would happen."

"Something like this?" Mary shook her head. "Nothing has happened."

"She's under the influence of a *bu* now. Next comes all kinds of trouble."

Mary knew that thoughts of Linda were racing through Silas's head. "Silas, please have more faith in Becky than that. She's not going to be led astray that easily. And, anyway, Noah isn't going to take her down the wrong path. I can vouch for his character. I've known him since he was born."

Silas turned back to stare out the window. Mary studied the hard set of his jaw and knew she had lost the argument. Her heart ached for him and his daughter. He had been so close to letting the past go.

"She won't be going to Pinecraft now, that's certain sure," he muttered. "I'm glad I never had a chance to tell her she could."

Becky flew inside, cheeks flushed with cold and happiness. "Noah asked to take me home!" she said as she clasped her hands together and tucked them under her chin. Her eyes were shining. Mary remembered what it had felt like to be young, when the most wonderful thing that could happen was for a handsome boy to take her home in his buggy. Of course, only one boy had ever asked her, and he had dumped her soon enough. But Mary had never forgotten how excited she had felt that he had noticed her. Her gaze shifted to Silas. Since he had come into her life, she had felt that excitement again, as if she was sixteen all over again.

And now, Silas was going to take that youthful joy from Becky.

"I did not give you permission," Silas said, each word dripping with authority.

Becky froze. The sparkle in her eyes disappeared. "But I thought I could go out now, like the other *youngies*." Her voice sounded so small that Mary wanted to scoop her in her arms and give her a good hug.

"Letting you go to youth group is a lot different than letting you ride home with a boy on his *rumspringa*."

"He's a *gut bu*." A look of panic spread across Becky's face. "He's not wild or anything."

"I could hear that stereo of his from inside the house."

"It's just a stereo. Lots of the *youngies* have them. He'll get rid of it when he gets baptized."

"*If* he gets baptized."

"*Daed!* How can you say that? Obviously, he's going to get baptized."

"You don't know that."

"Hardly anyone jumps the fence. You know how rare that is."

Silas's expression hardened. "Your *mamm* sure did."

"Noah isn't *Mamm* and neither am I! When are you going to see that!"

Mary put a hand on Silas's elbow. "Don't say anything you're going to regret," she murmured.

He opened his mouth, then closed it again. A few beats passed. "I shouldn't have brought up your *mamm*."

"Why not? You're thinking it whether or not you say it out loud. You may as well just go ahead and say it. You think I'm just like her. You think I'm going to do bad things and get in trouble. You think *I'm* bad."

"*Nee.*" Silas's expression shifted to frustration. "*Nee*, absolutely not."

"Then why do you act like it all the time?

I actually thought things were going to be different now. After you let me go with Martha this morning, I thought you finally trusted me. But I should have known better." Becky took off across the living room, her feet pounding the hardwood floor as she darted around the corner of the staircase and flew up the steps.

Silas let out a long, tired breath and collapsed into his chair. "*Vell*, that couldn't have gone worse." He dropped his head into his hands.

Mary could not agree more.

The next morning, Mary stood at the stove flipping cinnamon-pecan pancakes, waiting for Becky to come downstairs. She had already cooked the first round for Ethan, before Silas took him to school. As she slid her spatula underneath the bubbling batter, Mary heard the front door open with a whoosh of frosty air, then slam shut again. "Temperature's dropping," Silas announced from the living room. His black coat rustled as he hung it up, followed by the scrape of his boots on the floor as he took them off. He appeared in the kitchen doorway a minute later, cheeks ruddy with cold. "Looks *gut*."

"Danki."

They stood in awkward silence after that. Neither knew what to say to get past the tension between them. Finally, Mary couldn't take it anymore. "Today's the day the youth group is leaving for the tournament."

Silas stalked to his chair and sat down. "I know."

"You sound like you don't want to talk about it."

"I don't."

Mary fought to keep the emotion out of her voice. "Becky is hiding upstairs, devastated at missing out. Can't you reconsider?"

Silas just stared at the saltshaker in the middle of the table.

"I can think of a lot of *gut* reasons why

she should go, but I'm afraid you won't listen to any of them."

"You almost had me convinced before Noah drove her home." Silas sighed. "That didn't come out right. You made *gut* points. But in the end..." He threw up his hands. "She can't go all the way to Florida with a *bu* who wants to court her. I can only imagine what she might get up to, with him tempting her away from the faith."

"*Imagine* is the right word. You're imagining what *could* happen. A meteor could fall from the sky and hit us right now, too, but that doesn't mean it's going to. If you just let go and trust *Gott*—"

"I'm doing this so that she stays right with *Gott*."

"That has to be her choice. If you keep forcing it on her, she's far more likely to rebel."

Silas didn't answer. He just kept staring at the saltshaker, lost in his own world. Mary wondered if he was feeling remorse.

He seemed to be. She just wished he would let that remorse push him to change his mind, instead of burying it. Mary dropped the last pancake onto the serving plate and clicked off the gas burner. "Becky's breakfast is ready."

Silas pushed back his chair and stood up with a sigh. "I'll get her. She should have been down a long time ago to help. Being disappointed is no excuse for slacking off."

"I didn't mind cooking breakfast by myself this morning. She needs time to get over the disappointment. It's a big loss for a girl her age to miss out on a trip to Pinecraft."

Silas sighed again. "*Ya*, I guess it's okay to give her one morning off so she can deal with her emotions in private."

"I can put her plate aside for her if she needs more time."

"I'll go tell her that her breakfast is waiting and to *kumme* downstairs when she's ready."

Mary turned to face Silas. "Maybe you

could talk to her while you're up there, just the two of you."

"I wouldn't know what to say."

"Let her know you trust her, even though you're not letting her go to the tournament."

Silas looked like he was considering it for a moment, but then shook his head. "She won't believe me."

Mary took a deep breath. "Maybe she won't believe you because she's right. I don't think you do trust her. In which case, it's better not to lie. But you can at least tell her you love her and want what's best for her, even if she disagrees about what that is."

"I never said I didn't trust her. You just keep saying I don't."

"Because if you did, you'd let her go."

Silas grunted and left them room without disagreeing.

Mary's chest felt heavy as she stood at the counter. All she could think about was how much she wanted Becky to get to have fun with her friends. She remembered all the times her own father had forbade her from going out. The more he had kept her in, the shyer and more awkward she had become. He had never given her the chance to feel at ease around others or to learn how to be herself. Would Becky end up the same way?

The sound of footsteps pounding down the steps interrupted Mary's thoughts. "Mary!" Silas shouted. "She's gone. Becky's gone!" He shot into the kitchen and scrambled to a stop, his stocking feet sliding on the linoleum.

Mary froze, the spatula still in her hand. "What do you mean she's gone?"

"She's not in her room. I know she's not in the barn, because I put the horse back in his stall before I came in from taking Ethan to school. Where else could she be?"

Mary's stomach dropped to the floor. Becky wasn't in the house or the barn. And it was too cold for her to be in the yard. That could only mean one thing.

"She's run away," Mary whispered, not quite believing the words even as she spoke them aloud.

"Nee." The color drained from Silas's face. "That can't be."

"There's no other explanation. If she's not upstairs, she's gone for certain sure."

"She's not upstairs. I even checked my room, just in case."

They stared at each for an instant before they both registered what to do next.

"Let's go," Silas said. Mary had already started running for the door.

"The spatula."

Mary looked at her hand and realized she was still holding it. She didn't take the time to double back to the sink. She tossed it onto the table as she sprinted past. The spatula bounced up and clattered to the floor. Mary didn't stop to pick it up. She had to find Becky before something terrible happened.

Chapter Thirteen

Fear and anger pulsed through Silas with every beat of his heart. Becky had openly defied him to go to the tournament. "If we hurry, we can make it to the bishop's house and catch the youth group before they leave." His fingers fumbled with the metal buckles on Red Rover's harness as he struggled to hitch him up to the buggy.

Mary worked alongside him to save time. The sound of leather whispering against leather and the jangle of metal filled the still winter air. Their breaths rose in clouds of fog as they spoke. Silas knew it must be cold, but he was too anxious to notice.

His body felt numb and distant. He could not believe this was happening.

"You sound sure that she's with the other *youngies*."

He frowned and pulled the last buckle tight. "Where else would she be?"

Mary didn't answer. Her expression looked guarded.

"You don't think she's trying to leave for Pinecraft with them?" He jogged to the driver's seat without waiting for an answer.

Mary scrambled into the passenger side of the buggy, gathered the skirt of her dress around her and pulled the blanket they kept on the bench seat over her lap. Silas barely waited for her to get settled before slapping the reins. The buggy jerked forward. "Hold on," he said as he steered the horse out of the driveway. "We've got to hurry to get to the bishop's in time."

"Silas, I'm not so sure she's there."

Silas's expression hardened. "She's got to be." Another option slowly dawned on him. He sucked his breath in through his teeth. "*Ach, nee*. You think she's run off with Noah?" His stomach clenched even tighter. He had thought this couldn't be worse. It could be.

Mary frowned as she considered her response. "*Nee*. That's not what I meant."

Silas shook his head and ordered the horse to go faster. The buggy jolted as the animal quickened his pace, the wheels bumping along the uneven pavement. He stared into the distance, calculating how long it would take to get to Bishop Amos's farm at this speed. "She was so upset that I wouldn't let her see him. What if they've run off to get married? Or to jump the fence together?" Silas mind was racing from one unbearable scenario to another.

"Silas, please try not to panic until we know what's happened."

"How can I not panic? If ever there was a time to panic, it's now." He leaned forward in the seat, as if that could make the buggy go faster. Wind whipped past his face, nearly knocking his black winter hat from his head. He jammed it farther down on his forehead and scowled into the searing cold. "So where do you think she is, if you don't think she's with the youth group or with Noah?"

Becky slowly exhaled. "I don't know. But Becky's got a *gut* head on her shoulders. I don't think she's going to do anything rash."

"She's run away. You don't think that's rash?"

Mary readjusted the blanket on her lap with nervous fingers. "*Ya.* You're right. But I don't think she's run away to go against the faith."

"Then why do you think she's run away?"

Mary looked away. "To find the freedom you refuse to give her."

"What's she need freedom for, unless it's to do something against the faith? She doesn't need to go out unless it's to get into trouble. There's plenty to do in her own home."

Mary's head swiveled around to face him. Her eyes cut into him. "Silas, do you hear yourself right now? There's more to life than getting into trouble. She's sixteen years old. That's the age when a *youngie* just wants to have friends and have fun—fun that doesn't necessarily go against the *Ordnung*." Mary raised her eyebrows for emphasis. "You know, like playing volleyball."

Silas didn't like the way Mary was looking at him. Her expression had a distinct, I-know-more-about-this-than-you-do look. He wanted to argue, but something deep inside was afraid she was right. What was so bad about volleyball, after all? He quickly reminded himself what the problem was. "It's not playing volleyball that's so bad. It's what it might lead to. Being around all those *youngies* on *rumspringa*, she's sure to get tempted into something bad."

Mary sighed. "You had *kumme* so far.

I thought everything was going to be *oll recht*."

"I'm not the one who ran away," Silas said. He shoved down that little whisper inside that told him he had pushed his daughter away. "Her actions today have proved that I was right."

"Do you really believe that?"

Silas frowned as he looked straight ahead at the road stretching before them. He didn't have an answer.

When they reached the bishop's farm, Silas jumped out of the buggy before it had shuddered to a full stop. He hopped to catch his balance, then took off for the house. "Tie the horse to the fencepost for me," he shouted over his shoulder as his boots flew over the frozen ground. He prayed the charter bus taking the youth group to Florida had not already come and gone. Silas took the front porch steps two at a time. The wood creaked beneath his weight as he thudded across it, then he knocked hard on the door. He didn't wait for it to open. Instead, he stormed inside. The scent of woodsmoke and coffee greeted him, but he felt numb to the warmth and coziness of the bishop's tidy home.

"Hello?"

Edna appeared in a doorway alongside the entry hall, wiping her hands on her apron. The low rumble of excited voices filled the room behind her. "*Gude Mariye*, Silas!" She smiled broadly. "Have you changed your mind?" She looked past him, at the open door. "Is Becky with you?"

"*Nee*. I was hoping she was here with you." He took off his black felt hat and ran his fingers through his hair. "Not hoping… I mean…*vell*, it's better than the alternative."

Edna's face fell. "Silas, I don't understand."

"Becky's missing."

Edna inhaled sharply and darted back into the other room. She reappeared an instant later with her husband. Amos's normally cheerful face was taunt with worry. "What's this I hear? Becky's missing?"

"She wasn't in her bed this morning." Silas held up his hands. "She's gone."

"Is she here?" Mary's voice startled Silas. He had been so fixated on the situation he hadn't heard her at the doorway. She let herself in and closed the door behind her. He had forgotten to shut it.

Amos and Edna exchanged a quick, concerned glance. "She's not here, Silas," Amos said. "I wish she were." A sharp, icy wind howled against the farmhouse. As much as Silas hated the idea that Becky had disobeyed him to go to the tournament, the alternative was even worse. His knees felt weak but he forced himself to stay steady on his feet. He had to find his daughter before it was too late.

"Then I know where she is."

Amos and Edna looked surprised. "That's *gut*," Amos said. "I'll get my coat and go with you to get her."

"Nee." Silas shook his head. "I mean,

I know who's she's with. I don't know where they are. Headed to the *Englischers* in Lancaster, most likely."

"Who is she with?" Amos asked.

Silas face tightened in anger. He had known that Noah boy was bad news for his Becky. No one had believed him, but he had been right. "Noah."

Amos frowned and Edna looked confused. Amos put a hand on Silas's arm. "Silas, Becky isn't with Noah."

"How do you know?" Silas couldn't believe that. She had to be with him.

"He's here, in the living room with the other *youngies*, waiting for the charter bus to *kumme*."

Silas pushed past Amos and Edna and burst into the living room. His face must have reflected his anger, because the room fell silent and everyone turned to stare at him. Silas scanned the faces. Noah was there, leaning casually against the wall. He straightened up when Silas glared at him. "Where is she?" Silas demanded.

The room was so quiet that he could hear the crackle of the fire in the hearth. Noah's brow creased and he shook his head. "Who, Becky?"

"Of course I'm talking about Becky. Where is she? What are you two planning?"

Silas felt a small, steadying hand on his shoulder as Mary slid up beside him. Silas took a breath and tried to calm his tone. "Just tell me where she is. Please."

Everyone stared at Silas. He felt exposed and out of place. But nothing mattered except finding Becky.

Noah kept staring at him with a blank, confused expression. Finally, he shook his head and said, "Silas, I'm sorry, I don't know what you're talking about."

"You and my Becky. You're running away together, ain't so?"

Noah flinched. "I barely know her. Why would I do a thing like that?"

The teenagers looked from one to another as whispers began to spread throughout the room.

"Then where's Becky?"

"Silas, I told you. I don't know. Is she missing or something?"

Silas felt all the strength drain from his body. Could he really be wrong about this?

Mary spoke for him. "*Ya*, she's missing. But I'm sure there's a *gut* explanation for it. Silas is under a great deal of pressure right now to find his daughter. I'm sorry—"

"*Nee*, it's not your job to apologize for me, Mary." Her eyes jerked to his. He caught a flash of hope and relief in them. "I shouldn't have falsely accused you, Noah. I'm sorry." Silas covered his face with a calloused hand and rubbed downward. He had never felt so humiliated and afraid. But now was not the time for pride. He forced himself to look at the room of shocked faces. "Can you help me find her? Where do you think she might have gone?"

Becky's acquaintance, Martha, glanced around the room with a pained expression. When no one responded, she spoke up. "Silas, we never got to spend much time with her." She held up her hands, palms up. "How could any of us know where she went when we don't really know her?"

"But I thought you were friends."

"We never got a chance to be close enough to be friends."

Silas felt his decisions hit him like a brick. He had done this. He had isolated Becky to the point where she had no friends, no one to tell how she felt. And now, she had made a plan and kept it to herself. He had pushed her away, and no one knew where.

Silas spun around to face the bishop. "Help me organize a search."

Amos nodded, his face uncharacteristically stern. "Of course." He slid past Silas to address the teenagers. "Becky is one of ours and we won't leave until we know she's safe. Edna, would you please stay here in case Becky shows up? And let the charter bus driver know what's going on and tell him to wait. The rest of us will go out in groups and search. You *youngies* try to think of where you would go if you were running away and look there."

The crowd began to move quickly for the door.

"Wait," Silas said. "You're all on *rumspringa*, ain't so?"

Most of the teenagers nodded.

"Then could you please turn on your cell phones? That's the first thing *youngies* buy on *rumspringa*, so I know you have them."

The teenagers all looked at Bishop Amos. He nodded. "Since you're not baptized yet, I can allow it. Whoever's got a cell phone needs to use it to coordinate the search. Edna, check the phone shanty for messages every thirty minutes. And if any of you find Becky, let Edna know. Anyone who doesn't have a cell phone can check back here for updates."

The teenagers filed past, whispering to one another, faces taunt with anxiety. Silas motioned to Noah as he hurried by. "Noah."

Noah stopped short, his eyes still on the *youngies* ahead of him. *"Ya?"*

"Please *kumme* with Mary and me."

Noah did not look pleased with Silas's request. He frowned as he watched his friends rush out of the house. "Didn't think you'd want me anywhere near you."

"We may need your cell phone." Silas sighed. He didn't want to admit the other reason. "And you probably have a better idea of where she is than I do."

"I told you, I barely know her. I certain sure wanted to know her better, but..."

"I wouldn't let her go near you."

Noah cleared his throat and looked uncomfortable. "*Vell*, yeah."

Silas didn't want to waste any more time. He began walking out of the house. Noah and Mary followed. He could feel the tension in the air as they jogged to the buggy.

The yard was full of activity and nervous shouts as the teenagers called their *Englisch* drivers to come pick them up.

"She did say one thing," Noah said as he climbed into the back of the buggy.

Silas fumbled with the reins as he hurried to untie Red Rover from the fencepost. "What?" His heart thudded into his throat as he tugged the reins free and clambered into the driver's seat. "Anything you can think of might help."

"She mentioned that she wanted to go back home to Holmes County." Noah hesitated. "She said that if you wouldn't let her leave the house, then she couldn't stay here."

Silas swallowed hard. "She said that?"

"Yeah."

Silas and Mary looked at one another and the same words flew out of their mouths. "The bus stop." Silas nodded and Mary put her hand on Silas's arm as they held eye contact. They were in this together.

Then Mary turned her attention to a narrow dirt road that cut between two wheat fields. "That's the quickest way there."

Silas slapped the reins and the buggy jerked forward. "Becky's never been on her own before," he said as he leaned into the wind. He shook his head. "Anything could happen."

Mary kept her hand on Silas's arm.

He stopped himself from imagining all that could go wrong for her.

"Trust *Gott*," Mary said. "He can turn anything around for *gut*, even this."

The horse and buggy flew onto Main Street in a swirl of snow stirred up by the wheels. It took all of Silas's self-control to rein Red Rover into a slow walk to navigate the bustling thoroughfare. *Englisch* tourists chatted and smiled in their wool coats and thick scarves as they wandered the sidewalk, bags from the gift shop and bakery in their hands. They were going on with their vacations as if Silas's entire world wasn't falling apart.

They sailed past Beiler's Quilt and Fabric Shop, then the coffee shop, and finally reached the bus station. The building consisted of just one tiny room, but with the sunlight reflecting off the window, Silas couldn't make out who was inside. "Go," Mary said. "I'll tie Red Rover to the hitching post." She took the reins from Silas as he leapt from the seat. His throat felt dry and tight as he sprinted to the building and rushed inside.

Becky was there. Silas had never felt such relief in his life. She sat huddled on a plastic chair, her arms wrapped around herself in a sad hug. Her battered suitcase sat beside her feet. Thankfully, the room was clean and tranquil, just like the rest of downtown. There were no strangers or raised voices, just his daughter, looking despondent and alone in the quiet space. She stood up as soon as she saw him. *"Daed."* The color drained from her face. "Please don't be mad."

Silas rushed forward and had his arms around her before she could say another word. He hugged her as if they had been apart for years. He was surprised that she hugged him back just as fiercely. "I'm so glad to see you, *Daed*. I didn't want to go back alone."

Finally, Silas pulled away and picked up her suitcase. "Let's get out of here."

"I..." Becky looked down.

"*Kumme* next door to the coffee shop and we'll talk about it."

Becky didn't move. Her bottom lip trembled. "You're not mad at me?"

Silas considered his words carefully, then said, "I'm sad and afraid, but I'm not mad. I just want you to be safe. And happy. I want you to be happy, too."

Becky's expression shifted to surprise. "You do?"

"Of course, I do." He took her arm and gently steered her toward the door. "Vanilla latte, right?"

"With extra whipped cream."

"You got it."

Mary was standing in the parking lot,

blowing on her hands, nervously watching the doorway, when they emerged. Noah hung back beside the buggy, exchanged a quick nod with Silas and held up his cell phone. Noah would make sure everyone knew to call off the search. Becky didn't notice him, which was best for now. Silas needed time with her first.

Mary rushed toward them. "You're safe."

Becky threw her arms around Mary's neck. "You came for me."

"I certain sure did. You're my *dochder* now and I love you."

Becky's arms tightened and Silas heard a muffled sob. "I love you, too, Mary. I'm glad my *daed* married you."

Mary raised her head to look up at Silas. "I am, too." The strength of their feelings for one another passed between them in that long, unbroken gaze. Silas felt a renewed faith flow through him. Mary was right—*Gott* could turn anything to *gut*.

Silas wanted that moment to last forever, but it was freezing and he needed to get

Becky and Mary inside. "Let's head to the coffee shop to talk. There's a lot I need to say."

"Oll recht," Becky murmured. She pulled away from Mary and wiped her eyes. They were damp with tears.

"I'll wait for you in the fabric shop where it's warm. That way you can talk in privacy."

"*Nee*, Mary." Silas shook his head. "*Kumme* with us. You're part of our family now."

Mary glanced at Becky. Becky nodded and Mary smiled and slipped her arm in hers. "Let's go."

Mary could not stop clinging to Becky's arm. It felt so good to know she was here, safe and sound in Bluebird Hills. Becky leaned into her as they sat lost in their own world, despite the rumble of conversation around them from the Amish and *Englischers* gathered at their own tables, sipping warm beverages and nibbling cookies.

Silas came back from the counter carrying a cardboard tray with three disposable cups. He passed them out quickly and slid into a chair. "I made sure to get extra whipped cream," he said as Becky peeled off the plastic lid and blew across the top.

"Danki, Daed."

An awkward silence fell over the table now that it was finally time to talk. Mary could see the pain and regret in Silas's eyes, and the anxiety in Becky's.

"Where were you going?" Silas asked at last.

Becky kept her eyes on her vanilla latte. "Home to Ohio. I told you I was going back." Her eyes flicked up. "Where did you think I was going?"

Silas shook his head. "We'll talk about that later. First, tell me what you were thinking. It isn't safe for you to take off like that. You scared us half to death. If something had happened to you..." Silas cut off the sentence and clenched his jaw.

"We were worried," Mary explained. "If you had told us how you felt—"

"I did tell you. I told you both over and over again. I never kept it a secret. I said I'd go back to Holmes County and live with the Lantz cousins if you kept refusing to let me out of the house."

Silas pinched the bridge of his nose and squeezed his eyes shut. "You didn't tell us everything. You snuck out of the house so nobody would know what you were doing. But I admit that you told us you were planning on it." He dropped his hand and opened his eyes. "You tried to get me to see how bad it was for you here, shut up in the house away from the other *youngies.* I refused to listen. I'm sorry about that." He sighed. "I wasn't willing to see reality."

Becky narrowed her eyes in disbelief. "Did you just…apologize to me?"

"Ya." Silas gave her a sheepish smile. "*Daeds* can be wrong sometimes, ain't so?"

"For certain sure."

"Don't push it," he said, but his tone was playful. Becky smiled back. Then Silas's expression turned serious again. "Amish shouldn't have pride. I've got to admit when I'm wrong. I owe that much to *Gott* and to you."

"Wrong about everything? Even the tournament?"

Silas hesitated. "*Ya*, even that."

"Hard to admit, huh?"

"*Ya, ya*. Like I said, don't push it."

"And Noah? What about him? Do you trust me with him now?"

"Uh, *ya*. About Noah..."

"What about him?" Becky leaned forward.

Silas glanced at the door to the coffee shop, then back to Becky. "Never mind. Let's stay on topic, then we'll discuss Noah. First, we need to deal with the fact that you were wrong, too. Running away in secret wasn't the right way to handle this. It was a really dangerous thing to do."

Becky heaved a dramatic sigh. "*Ya*. I

know. But I was so hurt and angry that I didn't know what else to do. I just wanted you to trust me." She picked at the seam on her cardboard coffee cup. "I figured you didn't really want me around, anyway. Not when you think I'm so bad."

"Oh, Becky." Silas looked as if he had suddenly aged ten years. "I can't believe I made you feel that way. I am so sorry. I don't think you're bad. I've never thought that about you."

Becky shifted her gaze from the coffee cup to her father. "Then why do you treat me like I am?"

Silas's jaw flexed. There was a long, tense silence.

"Go ahead, Silas," Mary said. "It's *oll recht*. You can do this. You can tell her how you feel. I know you're strong enough, even if you don't think you are." She reached across the table and slipped her hand into his. He held it tightly.

"And here I was, thinking that I was

being strong by holding in my feelings and never showing my emotions."

"True strength is being brave enough to face your feelings and share them with others."

Silas gave a small, ironic smile. Then he took a steadying breath and looked directly in Becky's eyes. "I couldn't save your *mamm* from herself and I've been haunted by that every day of your life. I just thought, if I could save you..." He shrugged. "*Vell*, I guess it was a combination of wanting to protect you while also trying to redeem myself from all the guilt I felt for failing your *mamm*. I couldn't save her, so I certain sure had to do everything I could to save you."

Becky exhaled and slumped back in her chair. "This has never been about me. You never thought *I* was bad."

"*Nee*. And I shouldn't have put all this onto you. I'm sorry. I had *gut* intentions, but they led to hurtful actions. I'm sorry."

Becky nodded slowly. "I loved *Mamm*.

I'll always love her. But I don't want to be like her. I've worked hard my whole life to be the opposite of her. I want to have a *gut* Amish life. I don't want to go down the path she went down."

"I see that," Silas said softly.

"Do you really?" Hope filled Becky's eyes.

"*Ya*. I really do. And things are going to be different now, because of it."

The bell rang over the door of the coffee shop and Noah walked inside. His eyes shot immediately to their table.

Becky's attention cut to him. "Why is he here?" she whispered. "The youth group is supposed to be gone by now."

"I thought you might be planning to run off together."

Becky looked mortified. "*Daed*, how could you think that? Did you tell him that? *Ach, nee*, you did, didn't you? How could you that to me? What will he think of me now?"

"I'm the one who should be embarrassed, not you. I'm the one who got it all wrong. He knows that."

"*Daed*, he's coming this way!" Becky's face flushed bright red.

Noah strode to their table, his face tight with concern. He took off his black felt hat and turned it in his hands. "I couldn't wait any longer to see if you're okay." He glanced over to Silas. "I hope I'm not interrupting."

"*Nee*. It's *gut* you came."

Becky's face was still bright red. "Noah… I… I can't believe *Daed* thought… I never said anything…"

"It's true," Silas said. "She never said anything about running off with you. It was all my imagination running wild. I shouldn't have accused you."

Noah gave a quick nod to Silas, signaling his forgiveness.

"I never even said we were courting," Becky added in a small voice, but Mary caught the flicker of hope in her eyes.

Noah kept turning his hat in his hands.

"*Vell*, I'd like to court you, if that's *oll recht* with you and your *daed*."

"You would?" Becky straightened in her seat.

"I asked you to ride home from youth group with me, didn't I?"

"And you still want to walk out with me, even after all that's happened today?" She pressed a hand against her forehead. "I'm so embarrassed. Does everyone know?"

"We've all been out looking for you," Noah said.

"But the charter bus should have left by now."

"We delayed it."

"Why?"

"Because you're worth staying for. No one wanted to leave until we knew you were safe."

"But..."

Noah flashed a charming grin. "You're one of us now, Becky. Like it or not, we want you here, in Bluebird Hills." He cleared his throat and hesitated. "*I* want you here. I hope you'll stay."

Becky's face lit up. "I'll stay for certain sure, Noah."

Silas turned to Mary. "Now that that Becky's safe, I'd like to talk to you." He hesitated, then smiled. "Alone."

Mary's heart skipped a beat. Something in his eyes told her that what he had to say would be important.

Silas glanced out the window, to where a handful of teenagers from the youth group were gathered together, checking their cell phones. Another buggy pulled into the parking lot as he watched. "Noah, why don't you and Becky ride with the other *youngies* back to the bishop's house? Looks like they're about to head back there now. We'll follow behind you in our own buggy."

Noah smiled as he and Becky exchanged a quick glance. "I'd like that," he said.

Silas steered onto a turnoff that overlooked a lake surrounded by a field. The bright, winter sun sparkled off the water and the dusting of snow that coated the ground.

"Whoa," he said and the buggy rocked to a stop. He pulled the handbrake, then pointed ahead of them.

"Viola told me about this place and said that I should take you here sometime." He chuckled. "You know how she likes to meddle, but she was right about this. It's beautiful here."

"It is. You know that the bishop's farm is just over that hill, beyond the field?" Mary asked.

"*Ya*. I thought this would be a *gut* place to stop because we don't have much time before everyone leaves for Florida and we need to see them off. But this is too important to wait."

Mary gave him an encouraging nod. Nervous excitement swirled inside her.

"I just want to say…" Silas cleared his throat and turned to look at her. He moved the reins to his left hand, then reached for Mary's hand with his right one. His warm, reassuring touch sent a ripple of joy through her. She held her breath as she waited, hoping for the words she longed to hear.

He gazed into her eyes. "I love you, Mary. I'm not afraid to tell you anymore. And I'm not afraid to admit that I was wrong. You helped me see the truth, even though I didn't want to listen. Turns out you're not so mousy after all, huh?"

Mary's heart fluttered in her chest. She had never felt so happy or full. "You showed me how to find my voice," she whispered. "I never knew who I was before I met you." She leaned closer to him, barely able to believe the moment was real. "I love you, too, Silas. Answering that ad in *The Budget* was the best decision I ever made."

"For certain sure." Silas said. "And I don't just feel that way because you helped restore my family. I adore everything about you and I can't wait to spend the rest of my life with you."

Mary's pulse quickened as Silas closed his eyes and leaned into her. She closed her eyes as his lips met hers. It was her first kiss. And it had been worth the long wait because this breathtaking moment was with the man she loved with all her heart. The man who loved her in return.

The man who loved her for who she was, just as she had always longed to be loved.

Epilogue

South Florida's winter sun shone as bright as a Pennsylvania summer. Humidity shimmered in the sea breeze as Mary and Silas stood in the surf and warm water lapped over their toes. Mary squealed and hopped back a step. A little farther up the beach, Amish teenagers shouted and jostled on two sides of a volleyball net.

"I've got it!" Becky shouted. Mary and Silas watched as Becky dove for the ball. She managed to hurl it upward just before she hit the sand, face first. Silas flinched and Mary's hand flew to her mouth. But Becky bounced back up and shouted. "I knew I had it!" Then she shook the sand from her dress and hurried back into place.

"She really does have this," Mary murmured.

Silas grinned. "She *is* the best on the team."

"Go, Becky!" Noah shouted from the sidelines as he clapped for her. "You got this!"

"That's my sister!" Ethan yelled. Then he peeled the crust off his ham sandwich and threw it into the air. A cluster of seagulls screeched and swarmed, grabbing the bread before it hit the ground. Ethan laughed, then cheered for Becky as she hit the ball again.

"He's having a great time here," Mary said.

"*Ya*. I'm glad we came."

Mary looked over at Silas and raised an eyebrow. "You really mean that?"

"I do." He gave a sheepish shrug. "I was ready to let Becky *kumme* to Pinecraft without us, but I sure was glad when Amos suggested we chaperone."

"He knew you needed to ease into giving Becky this much freedom. And I think Becky is secretly glad, too. She's loving that you're here, cheering her on. It's *gut* for her to see that you support her."

Silas nodded and his eyes moved to his son. "It's been *gut* for Ethan, too. It's his first time at the beach, you know."

Mary turned to Silas. "The first of many?"

Silas put his arm around Mary and pulled her close. "I think we should chaperone this trip every year."

"I agree."

They paused, basking in the warm glow of the sun, listening to the shouts and cheers from the *youngies* nearby.

"Nothing is going to be the same, you know," Silas said after a while.

"*Nee*, it's going to be better than either of us ever imagined it could be."

Becky spiked the ball. It soared over the net and slammed into the sand.

"She's won the game!" Mary shouted.

Silas's arm tightened around her. "We've

all won," he murmured as he leaned down and kissed Mary on the top of her *kapp*.

Mary turned to look up into his eyes. "We all have, for certain sure."

One year later, the Hochstetler family was back at Pinecraft to watch Becky compete again, just as they had planned. As soon as they arrived, Mary and Silas arranged for Becky to watch Ethan so that they could take a long walk along the beach, just the two of them. Silas felt like the luckiest man in the world. There was nothing he enjoyed more than a quiet, romantic moment with the woman he loved.

Clear blue water stretched to the horizon, shimmering with gold from the setting sun. Clouds as pink as cotton candy filled the darkening sky.

Mary slipped her small, warm hand into his, a knowing smile on her lips. "I have something to tell you."

"What is it?" he asked as he tightened his grip on her hand. "Is everything okay?"

"Everything is *wunderbar*, Silas."

Silas smiled. *"Ya?"*

Mary laughed. "*Ya*. And not just because I'm head over heels for you."

Silas loved the way the corners of her eyes crinkled when she laughed.

Mary stopped walking and looked up at him. "We're going to have a *boppli*."

"A *boppli*?"

Mary laughed again. "*Ya*, that's what I said."

Silas was too overwhelmed with happiness to speak. He couldn't believe it. When words didn't come, he pulled Mary to him, kissed her, then picked her up and spun her around. "A *boppli*!" he shouted. "We're going to have a *boppli*!"

"Congratulations!" a stranger shouted from down the beach.

Silas grinned. He wanted to shout his joy and his love for his wife to the entire world.

Mary was still laughing when he set her bare feet back down on the white sand.

"A headstrong seventeen-year-old *and* a

boppli in the same house—are you sure you're ready for this?" Mary asked.

"Oh *ya*, I'm more than ready," Silas said. "What could be better than a baby of our own? A family of five sounds just perfect."

"Unless we become a family of six one day," Mary said.

"Even better," Silas said and smiled.

And he knew that smile would stay in his heart forever, alongside the never-ending love he held for his wife.

*****

Dear Reader,

After Mary King's appearance in *The Secret Amish Admirer* as Gabriel's single aunt, I wanted to give her a story of her own. Since she had been longing for a husband and children for many years, I loved the idea of sending her a ready-made family. But most importantly, I wanted Mary to find her voice and recognize her own worth. This is a realization that we all need to make. So, my hope is that you truly see how worthy of love you are.

Thank you for spending time in Bluebird Hills with me. I hope you return for my next book to wander the backroads of Lancaster County with favorite characters who have become friends.

In the meantime, you can find me at virginiawisebooks.com, on Facebook at VirginiaWiseBooks, and on Instagram at virginiawisebooks. I'd love to connect with you there.

Love Always,
Virginia